❀ TABLE *of* CONTENTS ❀

Nanea lives in Hawaii on the island of Oahu, so you'll see some Hawaiian words in this book. The meaning and pronunciation of these words are provided in the glossary on page 166.

Nanea's name is pronounced *nah-NAY-ah*. It means "delightful and pleasant."

A LAUHALA FAMILY

❀ CHAPTER 1 ❀

Nanea Mitchell lay in bed, pretending to sleep, while her big sister, Mary Lou, got ready. School was finally in session again after the Pearl Harbor attacks, and Mary Lou was going early to hang up "Welcome Back" banners at McKinley High.

After she finished her hair and dabbed a tiny bit of Tangee lipstick on her lips, Mary Lou grabbed the knitting bag she carried everywhere these days. She tiptoed out of their shared room as if she thought Nanea was asleep.

Nanea shifted, hugging her knees to her chest. She'd hardly slept the night before. It was finally February second, and until a few days ago, she had been so eager for this morning to come. Going back to school meant forgetting about blackouts and curfews and air raid drills. Sitting in Miss Smith's classroom at

❀ 1 ❀

Lunalilo Elementary, Nanea would be surrounded by friends and would get lost in spelling bees and flash cards and her teacher's lively stories. It was going to be wonderful.

But then everything changed. The Three Kittens—Nanea and her two best friends, Lily Suda and Donna Hill—were split apart. The military government had been in charge since the attack on Pearl Harbor, and it decided people like Donna and her mom were "non-essential civilians." They weren't helping the war effort, so they had to leave the island. Last Friday, Nanea and Lily had gone to the pier to say a final good-bye to Donna and her mother before they sailed off to San Francisco.

Nanea sighed heavily. Her dog, *Mele*, who had been sleeping on the floor next to her bed, stood on her hind legs to peer over the edge of the mattress. Nanea pulled back her quilt and patted the bed. Mele hopped up and snuggled against Nanea's side.

Nanea held her close, breathing in her doggy smell. Mele had gone missing after the attacks, and for two long weeks, Nanea had searched high and low for her. Since they'd been reunited, Mele didn't like to let

Nanea out of her sight. That was just fine with Nanea.

"I couldn't stand to lose you again," Nanea said, giving the dog a squeeze as she remembered that awful time. Mele shifted, knocking a newspaper clipping from the nightstand to the bed.

Nanea picked it up and studied the picture of herself with Lily and Donna and a group of their friends. Her family was so proud of Nanea for organizing a bottle drive for the Red Cross. The girls had collected over a thousand bottles so far. They'd had their picture taken for the newspaper. Nanea had even been interviewed by Miss Gwenfread Allen, a real reporter.

When the article came out yesterday, Papa taped a copy to the kitchen wall, and he sent another copy to Nanea's grandparents in Oregon. He'd even bought extra newspapers to give away to friends.

Nanea had smiled big for the newspaper photo, taken the day before Donna left. Now, when she looked at the picture, she couldn't think about the bottle drive. She could only think of how much she missed Donna. Mele thumped her tail on the bed.

"Okay, I'll read it to you again," Nanea said.

I recently had the pleasure of conversing with Miss Alice Nanea Mitchell—who goes by her Hawaiian name, Nanea—a poised and thoughtful young lady. Though Nanea was shy about taking credit, her friends assured me that she was the brains behind the highly successful bottle drive to benefit the Red Cross blood center. She says she was inspired by her brother's work in the hospital in the days after the attacks, when he carried bottles of blood to those in critical need. When she learned that Honolulu was long on blood donors but short on bottles, Nanea sprang into action.

Despite her accomplishments, this young lady confesses to losing sleep most nights. Each time she heads to her family's air raid shelter, she wonders if it's the real McCoy. She and her friends long for the return of their carefree island days. Days filled with jacks and jump rope and bike rides to the beach. Days where one's biggest concern was what flavor shave ice to order. While the war has required that we all make sacrifices, those paying the dearest price are our children.

Miss Allen's last words reminded Nanea again of how much she had given up, including one of her best friends. How could she go to school without Donna? She wished Papa were home so she could talk to him. He always made her feel better. But he was working another double shift at the Pearl Harbor shipyard. Nanea swallowed hard. Maybe she could say she was sick and Mom would let her stay home.

Mele licked Nanea's face.

"I know. It's time to get up." Nanea dragged herself out of bed and pulled on the school dress Mom had made her for Christmas. It was blue with pink and white flowers. Blue was Donna's favorite color. Nanea sat back down on her bed, thinking about Donna.

Nanea's seventeen-year-old brother, David, peeked his head through the doorway. "Breakfast is about ready," he announced. Then he looked at Nanea's face. "What's up, Monkey?" he asked.

"I don't know," Nanea answered, even though she did know. She was afraid if she told David, she'd start crying. And if she started, she might not stop!

David stepped into the room. "Shove over," he said.

Nanea made room for him on the edge of the mattress.

"You don't have to tell me," he said. "But does it

have something to do with that?" He pointed at the article, which had fallen to the floor.

"I know it's an honor to be in the paper," Nanea started. She leaned against David's strong shoulder, breathing in his familiar smell of Old Spice and jalopy grease.

"But?" he prompted.

"But it's like Miss Allen said. Too many things have changed." Nanea thought about how her island life used to be full of picnics at the beach, fishing with Papa, and playing outside in the long evening shadows. Now there was war. She couldn't stop the tear that trickled down her cheek. "The beaches are blocked by barbed wire; Papa's working all the time so we never go fishing anymore; we all have to sit in the dark night after night during the blackouts; one of my best friends is gone, and the other one . . ." Nanea's voice trailed off.

"What?" David asked.

Nanea sniffled. "Lily and I were walking home from Mrs. Lin's crack seed shop yesterday when someone yelled something not very nice at Lily—"

"—because she's Japanese." David finished Nanea's sentence for her.

Nanea nodded. "There are too many problems. And all of them are too big."

David's shirt was damp with Nanea's tears. "Monkey, I wish I could say that everything will get better soon. But nobody knows when this war will end. I'm sorry that my sweet little sis has to go through all this." He tapped her gently on the arm. "There is one thing I can tell you for sure."

Nanea tipped her head up to look into David's face. "What?" she asked, doubtfully. Her brother's Hawaiian name was *Kekoa*, which meant brave and strong. But not even David was strong enough to make the war stop.

"You don't have to face this alone. Your *'ohana*, your family, is here with you," he said. Then he picked up the small *lauhala* basket full of hair barrettes that Nanea kept on the dresser. "Think about this basket. One *hala* leaf is woven with another and another. Together, the leaves create something strong and sturdy. Just like our 'ohana."

Nanea reached for the basket and turned it around in her hands, thinking about how her mom and dad, brother and sister, and grandparents were part of the weaving of her life. "You're right, David."

"Of course I am," David teased, ruffling her hair. "We all have to work together to win this war. The more everyone helps, the sooner things can get back to normal." David stood up. "I can tell you one more thing for certain."

Nanea returned the basket to the dresser. "What?"

"Mom is going to fuss if we aren't at the breakfast table right away." He smiled his movie star smile at her, tapping the door frame as he left the room.

Nanea clipped a barrette in her hair. "I guess I could manage a little something for breakfast," she said to Mele. "And I know *you* can always eat." She picked up her dog and cuddled her close. Nanea tried not to miss Donna, but it was impossible. Her friend was as much a part of the weaving of her life as Mele was.

RIGHT-HAND GIRL

anea had just finished brushing her teeth when Lily knocked at the door. "Are you ready?" Lily called.

"Yes." Nanea swung her gas-mask bag over one shoulder and her book bag over the other. Inside the book bag was a woven bookmark that Nanea had made for Miss Smith. Since her teacher loved stories, Nanea knew she would love this welcome-back present.

Mom kissed the top of Nanea's head. "Do your best today," she said.

With Mele trotting behind, the girls walked down Fern Street. Nanea still wasn't used to the gloom that had settled on their neighborhood from all the windows being covered. Some had been painted black, and some were lined with heavy dark curtains to keep light from leaking out during the nightly blackouts. Though most neighbors' curtains were open in the daytime, they still framed the windows like frowns.

When the girls turned onto Pumehana Avenue, Nanea couldn't keep from looking over at Donna's house. She so wished there was a blonde-haired girl on the front steps, chewing away on a piece of Bazooka bubble gum, waiting to walk to school with them.

Lily looked, too. "I miss Donna," she said, shifting her gas-mask strap to the other shoulder with a sigh.

"I'm going to write her as soon as I get home from school today," Nanea said. "I'll tell her everything that happened."

"Great idea!" Lily stepped over a gecko that was sunning itself on the sidewalk. "I will, too."

Across the street from the school, Nanea stopped to say good-bye to Mele. "See you this afternoon, girl." Nanea knelt down to give Mele a hug, but as she tried to stand, the weight of the gas mask and the book bag pulled her right over. She was flat on her back.

"Help!" Nanea flailed her arms.

"You look like a pill bug," Lily said, reaching out a hand to help. She began to giggle.

"I feel like one!" Nanea got to her feet, laughing as

well. It felt good to laugh. "Did I get any dirt on my dress?" She turned around and Lily patted at the skirt.

"Good as new," Lily pronounced.

"I hope so." Nanea grinned. "It *is* new!"

Mele had been sitting, head cocked, watching the girls.

"I know. Pretty silly, right?" Nanea said to her dog. "Now, you head on home."

Mele hesitated. This would be the first time they'd been apart all day since Nanea found Mele after the bombing.

"It'll be okay," Nanea said gently. "I'll be home before you know it."

Reluctantly, Mele trotted off, and the girls crossed the street and entered the school building. Normally, Nanea and Lily would've hurried up the worn wooden stairs to their classroom on the second floor. But the stairs were now blocked by yellow ropes that were tied between the bannisters. Up above, workers were still repairing the library and classrooms that had been damaged by the fire on December seventh. That was one more thing that had changed because of the war.

The girls made their way to a smaller room on the

first floor and squeezed through the aisles. They took
the same seats near the window that they'd had in
their old classroom, and hung their gas masks from the
backs of their chairs. Miss Smith wasn't there yet, so
Nanea hurried to place the neatly wrapped bookmark
on her teacher's desk. On her way back to her seat, she
smiled to think how surprised Miss Smith would be
and how much she'd like the present. She'd probably
use it right away!

More kids wandered in, including a girl Nanea
hadn't seen before. Finally, Miss Smith sailed into the
classroom. "Good morning, scholars," she said.

"Good morning, Miss Smith," Nanea and her classmates answered.

"Oh my goodness!" Miss Smith pressed her hands
to her cheeks. "To see your smiling faces is a dream
come true."

The cares and worries of the past months slipped
off Nanea's shoulders. Miss Smith was like Superman,
swooping in to save them all from the troubles of the
world. Miss Smith asked Lily to lead the flag salute.
Then she took attendance. The new girl answered,
"here," when Miss Smith called out, "Dixie Moreno."

"Dixie, we're so glad you've joined our class,"
Miss Smith said. "Would you like to tell us a bit about
yourself?"

Dixie wore a short brown pageboy haircut and a
slightly crooked smile. She stood up confidently at her
desk. "I've moved here from Maui because my dad has
a new job at Wheeler Airfield. We're living with my
aunt and uncle for now. I love tap dancing, and when
I'm older I'm getting three dogs." She smiled. "I can't
have pets now because my aunt's allergic." She sat
down.

"Welcome, Dixie," Miss Smith said. "I think you'll
find we're a friendly crew."

Nanea didn't feel completely friendly toward Dixie,
who was sitting where Donna should be. But Nanea
did feel terrible that Dixie wanted a dog and couldn't
have one. She gave her a smile, and Dixie smiled back
but the smile turned into a yawn, which Dixie covered
with her hand.

"Now, before we begin our lessons, I need to
make new classroom job assignments," Miss Smith
announced. As she called off names, she had each
person come forward to get a small cardboard tent to

place on his or her desk. The tents announced which job the student had been given. Nanea waited patiently to hear her name. Not everyone would get an assignment today. The tasks would rotate in a few weeks. But since Miss Smith always called Nanea her "right-hand girl," Nanea knew she would get a job on the first day back.

Miss Smith assigned a desk inspector, attendance runner, chalkboard cleaner, and milk-money collector. Nanea was happy that Lily got to be supply chief. Lily loved keeping track of all the paper and crayons and glue in the storage cupboard.

Miss Smith picked up the last tent. "The War Stamps monitor will be in charge of the weekly War Stamps sale for the rest of the school year. As you all know, every stamp helps the war effort, so this job is very important," Miss Smith explained.

Now Nanea knew why Miss Smith hadn't called her name yet. She was saving the War Stamps monitor job for her right-hand girl.

Miss Smith smiled. "This job goes to . . ."

Nanea sat up nice and tall.

"Dixie Moreno." Miss Smith beamed at the new girl.

"I'll do my very best," Dixie said. She held her head high as if a halo sat on top of it.

A little crab of jealousy pinched at Nanea. Why would Miss Smith give that big job to the new kid? Someone who didn't even know everyone's names? Someone who liked tap dancing? It wasn't fair.

Miss Smith cleared her throat. "Scholars, we have a very exciting opportunity. If ninety percent of the class buys stamps, we can earn a Minuteman flag." She clasped her hands together. "Just imagine that special flag flying over our school, showing Honolulu, Oahu—the world—that we are doing our part here at Lunalilo to help the war effort!"

The class murmured with excitement. "I've seen a real Minuteman flag," Albert Ogawa announced. "They're nifty."

Miss Smith's eyes sparkled and her cheeks turned rosy with excitement. "I know many of you have uncles and brothers and fathers who are serving in the military. My own brother is in the Army Air Forces. I wonder if you scholars would like to dedicate our stamp drive to those brave men." She took a picture frame from her desk and turned it around so the class could

see her brother's photo. He was dressed in a snazzy
uniform and smiled proudly.

Nanea glanced around the room. She could tell
from her schoolmates' faces that they all felt as she did.
They would not let Miss Smith, or her brother, or any of
their family members, down. They would do their part
for the war effort and earn a Minuteman flag!

When the lunch bell rang, Lily grabbed her paper
sack and picked up her jacks set. "Shall we ask the new
girl to join us?"

Nanea didn't really want to invite Dixie, but her
mother had taught her to always be welcoming to
someone new. She glanced over at Dixie, who had
pulled a book out of her bag and was unwrapping a
sandwich at her desk. "It looks like she's staying in,"
Nanea said.

"Oh, okay." Lily followed Nanea out of the room.

Outside, Nanea reached into her lunch sack. Mom
had made her a bologna sandwich. Donna's favorite. But there wouldn't be any trading today because
Donna wasn't there. "What do you think Donna's

getting for lunch on the ship?" Nanea asked. "Do you think it's something special for their last day at sea?"

Lily put a straw in her milk bottle. "I bet she gets chocolate cake for dessert." That was Lily's favorite.

"With ice cream!" Nanea added. She imagined Donna and her mother all dressed up in the ship's elegant dining room, curling their pinkies as they sipped tea from delicate china cups. Someday Nanea would take a trip on a Matson liner and dine on fancy meals with rich desserts. She peeked in the bottom of her lunch sack. Until then, she'd be happy with Mom's homemade peanut butter cookies.

When she and Lily went back to class after lunch, Dixie was still at her desk, but now Miss Smith was sitting next to her. Dixie was showing their teacher something in the book she was reading. Dixie and Miss Smith both laughed.

The bologna sandwich turned to lead in Nanea's stomach. Miss Smith was acting like *Dixie* was her new right-hand girl! Nanea felt the little crab-pinch of jealousy again.

Miss Smith kept the class hopping the rest of the afternoon. She gave them a math pop quiz, and then they had a boys-against-girls spelling relay. Nanea's word was "dream," which she quickly spelled correctly. She ran back to her desk to tag Dixie. Dixie's word was "sitting," but she left out the second *t* so the girls lost the relay. Dixie didn't even say she was sorry. She just yawned like she was bored with it all.

When the bell rang at the end of the day, the students jumped up to gather their belongings.

"Oh, Nanea," Miss Smith called. "Would you mind staying after a moment?"

Nanea smiled. "Wait for me," she said to Lily.

Lily nodded. "I'll be out front."

Nanea approached the teacher's desk expectantly. Miss Smith had probably been thinking about the big mistake she'd made with the War Stamps monitor assignment. Now everything would be set to right.

"Thank you so much for this beautiful gift." Miss Smith held up a book with Nanea's bookmark peeking out. "I've already put it to good use."

"I thought you would like it," Nanea said, pleased that she knew her teacher so well.

Miss Smith leaned toward Nanea, as if sharing a secret. "You are my right-hand girl," she said. "So I have a very important job for you."

"I can do it!" Nanea said confidently. That Minuteman flag was as good as won. Nanea could already picture it flying over the school, with Miss Smith beaming at her for doing such a good job.

Miss Smith fiddled with her earring. "Dixie was feeling a little sad today so I let her stay inside for lunch. But I know she'd have more fun playing outside. I'd like you to be her special buddy. Help her get to know her classmates. Make her feel welcome."

"Dixie?" Nanea blinked. Miss Smith wasn't changing her mind about the War Stamps monitor job. She wanted Nanea to buddy up to a bad speller!

"Thank you, dear." Miss Smith pushed her chair back from her desk. "I knew I could count on you."

POSTER PROBLEMS

O n Friday morning, Nanea folded her letter to Donna and slid it into an envelope. Then she picked up the three-cent stamp Mom had given her. "This is the second letter I've written to Donna since she left," Nanea said. She licked the stamp and pasted it to the envelope. "I wonder why I haven't gotten one from her yet."

Mom wrapped Nanea's peanut butter sandwich in wax paper. "Be patient, honey. Donna only left a week ago. And things are slow at the post office because the Army's censoring the mail." Mom motioned at Mary Lou to put away her knitting and eat her breakfast. "Every letter going out and coming in has to be read by an official before it's delivered."

Mary Lou put her yarn and needles down and squeezed lemon juice over her papaya. "And there are all kinds of rules about what you can put in a letter."

"You can't even write about the weather," David added. "If the enemy got ahold of the mail, that information could help them plan an attack." He stood up and cleared his breakfast things. "I'm heading out. I'll be home late because of that training for my new job."

Nanea took a bite of toast. "Isn't working at the hotel enough?" David already had a job at the Royal Hawaiian.

"There's not much of a need for bellboys these days," he answered.

Nanea sighed. The only people coming to the island now were sailors and soldiers, not tourists. That was a big change, not just for the hotels, but for people like Nanea's next-door neighbor, Auntie Rose. She used to make *leis* to sell to visitors at the dock on Boat Days. But Boat Days were no more, and most of the flower fields were being turned into Victory Gardens. So Auntie Rose and the other lei sellers went to work weaving camouflage nets for the Army. All because of the war.

David smiled his movie star smile. "Anyway, now I can help Uncle Sam by delivering important messages!"

"That does sound like an essential job," Nanea said.

"I wish I could do more." David picked up his books and lunch sack. "Two more guys from my class have joined up."

Mary Lou nodded. "Every day they announce the names at school."

"You're doing plenty," Mom said to David. She kissed him good-bye. "I'll keep some supper warm for you."

Nanea could hear the engine of David's old jalopy revving up as she finished her toast. She knew Mom didn't like it when David talked about the people who had enlisted in the Army.

After Mary Lou cleared her dishes and left the kitchen, Nanea asked, "Do you worry that David will join up, too?"

Mom handed Nanea her lunch sack. "Let's not borrow trouble," she said. "Just do your best at school today. Is that letter ready to go?"

Nanea gave the letter a kiss for good luck. "Get there as quickly as you can," she told it. Then she handed the letter to Mom, and she and Mele ran to meet Lily.

Nanea couldn't wait to tell Lily the great idea she'd

had while she was trying to fall asleep in her pitch-black room. She'd been thinking about the Minuteman flag, and how her class wanted to work together to earn one and help the war effort. But buying War Stamps wasn't the only way to help. That's when Nanea came up with a doozy of an idea.

"I want to start a club: the Honolulu Helpers!" she exclaimed to Lily.

"Good name," Lily said. "What will the club do?"

"Help the war effort in Honolulu. We'll keep up with the bottle drive, of course," Nanea said. "And we could babysit again while moms take first-aid lessons. We can volunteer to work in Victory Gardens, and bake cookies, and serve meals, and even help in hospitals."

"Can I join?" Lily asked with a smile.

"Of course! And Patricia and Linda and Judy and Makana." Nanea began to list schoolmates' names.

"And Dixie?" Lily asked.

Nanea paused and scratched her neck. She had tried to be a buddy to Dixie. She had asked Dixie to join them for lunch every day that week, but Dixie had said no to every invitation and chosen to stay inside instead. Sometimes Dixie's head was on her desk and her eyes were closed when the rest of the class came in. Dixie often yawned through the afternoon lessons. "Dixie doesn't seem like a joiner," Nanea finally said. "Besides, she's probably pretty busy being War Stamps monitor. Oh, that reminds me: I thought of a way to help her with that job."

"How?" Lily nudged Nanea so she wouldn't step on a gecko.

"You know how I'm good with words and you're good with art?" Nanea asked.

Lily nodded.

"So we'll help Dixie with the War Stamps drive by making posters!" Nanea tugged her gas-mask strap to keep it on her shoulder. "I'll come up with a slogan, and you'll draw the pictures." She did a hop jump. "That will inspire our classmates!"

"But Dixie's the War Stamps monitor," Lily said. "Isn't she supposed to do things like that?"

Nanea made a face. "Yes, but she's new. Besides, Miss Smith asked me to help her."

Lily rubbed her nose. "Is this what Miss Smith had in mind?" she wondered.

"It is," Nanea said. She was Miss Smith's right-hand

girl. She was sure she knew what her teacher meant.

When they got to class, Lily handed Miss Smith a note. "I have a dentist appointment today," she said.

"I'm sorry you'll miss the first chapter of our read-aloud," Miss Smith said. "But I hope you have a good checkup!"

The morning dragged for Nanea. She was so excited about the Honolulu Helpers. The moment the first recess bell rang, she bolted outside, gathering up her friends.

The girls loved the idea. "Can we have uniforms?" asked Makana.

Nanea hadn't thought of that. "I guess so," she said. The group talked, and they finally settled on white dresses with red neck scarves. Everyone had a white dress, and they decided they could make neck scarves.

"What will our first project be?" asked Linda. "I mean, after we make the scarves?"

Nanea *had* thought of that. "Valentine's Day is coming up. We could make cards for soldiers."

The girls all agreed. "This is going to be so much fun," said Makana.

Nanea smiled. Fun *and* a big help to the war effort.

After lunch, Lily left for her dentist appointment and the rest of the class settled in with paper and crayons for the read-aloud. Miss Smith always let them draw and doodle during read-alouds.

Miss Smith perched on her reading stool in the front of the room. "This is *The Family from One End Street*, written and illustrated by Eve Garnett. I brought this book from home since we are without a library for the time being." Miss Smith looked sad, but her voice was cheerful as she began to read. *"There were a great many Ruggles children—boys and girls, and a baby that was really a boy but didn't count either way yet."*

Nanea rolled a crayon back and forth on the desk, listening to the lively story about a family with seven children.

"There are seven of us in my aunt's house," Dixie exclaimed. She stifled a yawn. "It's awfully noisy."

"I imagine it would be." Miss Smith smiled sympathetically at Dixie.

As Miss Smith read on, Nanea got caught up in the story. She jumped when Miss Smith closed the book.

"We'll leave it there until Monday," Miss Smith said. "But you may have five more minutes to finish your drawings before we move on to math."

Nanea added the final touches to her picture. She'd drawn three girls under the mango tree in her back-yard, each reading a book. One of them was blowing a big pink bubble. Nanea decided she'd send the drawing to Donna. As she put her crayons away, she looked over at Dixie's desk. She'd drawn a picture of Mickey Mouse. It was good, even if it was kind of lopsided.

Dixie finished coloring in the ears, then wrote "Make Mickey happy. Buy War Stamps" at the bottom.

"What's that?" Nanea asked.

Dixie added a red bow tie. "A poster to get kids to buy War Stamps. "

"But Lily always does the art for our classroom." Nanea's face flushed with jealousy. "She and I were going to make posters when she gets back from the dentist." Nanea snatched the drawing away.

Dixie grabbed it back, and a big corner of Mickey's ear tore off. "My poster!"

"Nanea. Dixie." Miss Smith's voice was stern. "Out in the hall."

Nanea had never been sent to the hall. She'd never been in trouble at school before—not until Dixie arrived. And now here she was in trouble the first week back at school.

Miss Smith sat Dixie on the floor on one side of the classroom door and Nanea on the other. "I certainly didn't expect this sort of trouble from either of you." Miss Smith looked at Nanea, and Nanea felt sick with shame. "I'm going to get your classmates started on their math problems. I'll be right back."

Nanea's head fell to her knees. Miss Smith was disappointed in her. What if she sent a note home? Mom and Papa would be disappointed in her, too. Papa was always telling her to think first before acting.

A few minutes later, the door opened again. "Please tell me what happened," Miss Smith said.

"I want to do a good job as War Stamps monitor," Dixie said. "I thought a poster would remind everyone to bring in their dimes, so I made one."

"I see." Miss Smith nodded. "That sounds like a fine goal, don't you think, Nanea?"

"But *Lily* is the class artist," Nanea said. "She should make the poster."

"It seems to me that we have room for more than one artist," said Miss Smith. She bent down toward Nanea. "Is there something you'd like to say to Dixie?" she asked kindly.

Nanea tugged at the hem of her dress. "I'm sorry about your poster," she said.

"Maybe we can tape that piece back on," Dixie said.

"All right, girls." Miss Smith stood up. "I know I can count on you to get along from here on out. Let's go back to class."

The girls stood, and then Miss Smith turned and put her arm around Dixie's shoulder.

Nanea felt tears sting her eyes, and she bit her lip to keep from crying. As Miss Smith walked Dixie back to her desk, Nanea went to the supply cupboard to get the cellophane tape. She could tape Mickey's ear back together, but she didn't know how she would fix the trouble she had gotten into.

TOOTSIE POP
WISHES

The next morning, Nanea stood outside her grandmother's *lanai*, waiting for *Tutu's* invitation to hula class. She hadn't told anyone about the poster problem, and it weighed her down like a big boulder.

"*Makaukau?*" Tutu asked the girls if they were ready to dance.

Nanea answered, *ae*, yes, along with the other dancers, but she didn't feel ready. She was still upset about what had happened the day before. So upset, she miscounted the number of *kaholo* steps during the warm-ups. And she started with her hands down instead of at her head for "Sweet Leilani."

Tutu stopped the music. "Hula isn't just about moving one's hands and feet," she said gently. "It's about telling a story." She looked thoughtfully into Nanea's

eyes. "Your mind must be on the story," she advised
before starting the music again.

Nanea felt her face turn pink.

After class, as the other girls gathered their things,
Nanea thought about telling Tutu about the incident at
school. But before she could say anything, a car horn
honked out front. It was David, there to take them to
Pono's Market. Nanea worked at her grandparents'
store every Saturday now, and she even helped out a
few days after school, too.

As Nanea climbed in the backseat, David helped
Tutu into the car. Then he got behind the wheel. "One
good thing about working for Uncle Sam," David said
as he drove, "is getting extra gas rations!"

People were driving less and walking more or
taking the bus, because gasoline was now being
rationed on the islands. It was another change because
of the war.

"Thank you," Tutu said as David helped her out of
the car at the market.

"Have a good day at work," added Nanea.

"You, too," David said. He hopped back in his
jalopy and drove off.

"Aloha!" Nanea's grandfather called out the minute Nanea and Tutu stepped inside the market. "There's our famous girl!" *Tutu Kane* gestured toward the wall where a set of war posters encouraged people to "Dig On for Victory" and "Can All You Can: It's a Real War Job." Next to them was a copy of the newspaper article about Nanea and her friends.

"Tutu Kane is so proud, he about popped all the buttons off his favorite aloha shirt." Tutu chuckled.

Nanea cringed as she tied on the Pono's Market apron she'd gotten for Christmas. What would her family say if they knew she'd gotten in trouble at school? "I'll start dusting," she said, quickly moving away from the front counter.

Nanea started pulling cans and jars from a nearby shelf. She was cleaning with a feather duster when the bell over the front door jingled.

"Hello, Nanea," Mrs. Robida, one of the market's regular customers, called as she stepped into the store. "It's so nice to see you working today."

Nanea smiled, smoothing the front of her apron. "May I help you with something?" she asked.

"Some fabric for a quilt," Mrs. Robida said. Nanea

pulled down several bolts of cloth before Mrs. Robida found what she wanted. Tutu took the big shears and cut exactly what Mrs. Robida asked for.

Nanea helped another lady find Saloon pilot crackers. Then a teenage girl wanted some fishing line, and after that, Mr. Lopez from the bakery next door came in for baking powder.

"You've got a good helper here," Mr. Lopez told Tutu Kane.

"Don't I know it!" Nanea's grandfather agreed.

Between customers, Nanea put the canned goods back on the dusted shelves. Tutu Kane had written sale prices on small signs, which Nanea displayed next to each product. The Libby sliced beets were fourteen cents a can. The guava jelly was twenty-nine cents a pint. One sign in Tutu Kane's neat printing read, "Kamehameha salmon: a bargain at thirty-three cents a can." As she taped the signs to the shelves, Nanea thought about Dixie and the Mickey Mouse poster on the classroom bulletin board, torn ear and all.

When Tutu Kane locked up the store at five o'clock, Tutu came to admire Nanea's work. "My, you'd think this was a fancy Piggly Wiggly grocery store!" She

shook her head in amazement. "Look at those spar-
kling shelves." Tutu took the lid off a jar of penny
candy. "Such hard work deserves a reward."

Nanea chose a grape Tootsie Pop and slowly pulled
off the wrapper.

"You've been awfully quiet today," Tutu Kane
observed as he flipped through receipts. "Everything
okay?"

"I miss Donna." Nanea ran her tongue over the
ridge in the middle of the sucker. "Sometimes I even
think I smell her bubble gum."

Tutu sighed. "It is hard when someone you love
is far away." She turned to tap the article on the wall
behind her. "What Miss Allen said is so true. This war
has been hardest on you children. You don't deserve
such grown-up worries." She straightened a display
of postcards on the counter. "That's why Tutu Kane
and I are so impressed with all you're doing. You're
managing the bottle drive, dancing at the USO shows,
helping here at the market, and now you've started the
Honolulu Helpers. All that and you're still such a good
student. We're so proud of you."

Nanea winced. She couldn't stand it anymore. She

had to tell somebody. "You wouldn't be proud of what I did yesterday," she confessed.

"Oh?" Tutu stopped straightening.

Nanea told her what happened. "I was only trying to be Dixie's buddy, like Miss Smith asked." She wiggled her bare toes. "None of it would have happened if Miss Smith had given me the War Stamps monitor job."

Tutu nodded, thoughtful. "So it's Miss Smith's fault that you tore Dixie's poster?"

"No. That was my fault." Nanea dropped her head. "I was trying to *kokua* for Dixie, but she wouldn't let me help her."

"Hmmm." Tutu patted Nanea's back. "How did you know that Dixie wanted your help making posters? Did she tell you?"

"No." Nanea sighed. "But Dixie is new. She doesn't know our school or anything about it. Why did Miss Smith pick her to be the War Stamps monitor?"

"You would have been good at that job, I'm sure," Tutu said. "But I wonder if Miss Smith's idea of kokua was giving Dixie the job. It has probably helped her get to know her classmates. Perhaps she's not so lonely for the friends she left behind."

Tutu Kane pointed at the newspaper clipping on the wall. "You have your story, *keiki*. Dixie has her own. Maybe you could discover what it is."

Nanea nodded slowly. Then she lowered her voice to a whisper. "I don't think I'm Miss Smith's right-hand girl anymore." She told her grandparents about seeing her teacher put an arm around Dixie's shoulder.

Tutu's face was kind. "That's the wonderful thing about love," she said. "There's always enough to go around. When Mary Lou was born, I loved David just as much as ever. And when you arrived, that didn't change my love for your brother or your sister." Tutu patted her chest. "Hearts can grow big enough for all the people in our lives. It's the same for teachers as it is for tutus."

Nanea took a deep breath. Tutu's words made her feel so much better, and what Tutu Kane said had given her an idea. Nanea waved the Tootsie Pop as if it were a magic wand. "May I take Dixie one of these to show her I want to be her friend?"

"Good idea." Tutu opened the lid on the candy jar again. "And take one for Lily. Old friendships are sweet, too."

DIXIE'S STORY

CHAPTER 5

Nanea hopped out of bed and dressed more quickly than usual.

"You're awfully eager for a Monday morning," Mary Lou grumbled, slowly sitting up in bed. "What's the hurry?"

"It's War Stamps day," Nanea answered. She patted the dime in her skirt pocket, her pay from working at Pono's Market. She was going to be the first in line to buy a stamp. More importantly, she was going to start over with Dixie and really listen to her story.

Nanea was happy to see Papa at the kitchen table, drinking coffee. "You're back to just working one shift!" Nanea exclaimed, throwing her arms around her father's neck and squeezing two times. It was their secret code for "buddies forever."

He squeezed back. "Yes—the graveyard shift for

the next few weeks," he smiled. Papa would go to work after dinner and come home in time for breakfast. It was the shift he usually worked, and it meant he slept during the day while Nanea and David and Mary Lou were at school.

Nanea's egg and toast and mango jam tasted even better with Papa sitting at the table.

Nanea was first in line to buy a War Stamp that morning. After she gave Dixie her dime, Nanea said, "Would you have lunch with me and Lily today? Please?"

Dixie looked surprised, but she said yes.

When the lunch bell rang, the girls went outside and sat at a table in the shade. Instead of opening her lunch sack, Dixie sat rubbing her eyes.

"Do you feel okay?" Nanea asked.

Dixie pushed her lunch sack to the middle of the table and rested her head on her arms. "I'm too tired to eat," she said.

Lily nodded. "Sometimes I have a hard time sleeping because of the blackouts, too. I lay awake listening for the sounds of planes," she confessed.

Nanea agreed. "The grown-ups tell us not to worry, but how can we help it?" She thought about all the nights she tossed and turned, wondering if there would be another attack.

Dixie lifted her head. "That used to be my problem," she said. "But now I can't sleep because I have to share a room with my three little cousins. They're too young to go to school. They think we're having a pajama party every night." Dixie yawned again.

"I remember when Tommy was a baby," Lily said. "He kept us awake a lot."

"Dad says housing is hard to find and that my aunt is good to take us in, so I don't want to complain." Dixie halfheartedly opened her lunch sack, pulled out a banana, and began to peel it. "But there's something else," she sighed.

"You can tell us," Nanea said.

"It's hard being at my aunt's for another reason. She's my mom's sister." Dixie set the banana down. "Every time I look at her, I see my mom. She even sounds like my mom."

Nanea and Lily exchanged glances. Neither one

of them knew what to say. Finally, Nanea said softly, "Where is your mom?"

Dixie shrugged. "She won a singing contest when I was five years old. The prize was a ticket to Los Angeles to try out for a movie." Dixie put the uneaten banana back in her lunch sack. "I guess she likes being in the movies better than she likes being a mom."

Nanea set down her own sandwich. "That's really sad," she said.

Lily gave Dixie a sweet rice cake from her lunch. "Have my *mochi*," she said.

"It's hard," Dixie admitted, biting into the mochi. "Mom writes me once a month, and when I'm older, I get to go visit her." She looked at the mochi. "I just miss her so much," she said sadly.

The girls finished the rest of their lunches without saying much. Then they picked up their wrappers and bags and started walking to the playground. "Wait," Nanea said. She pulled a purple Tootsie Pop from the bottom of her lunch bag and handed it to Dixie. "I really am sorry about the poster."

"I know," Dixie nodded. She unwrapped the sucker. "Thanks. Grape's my favorite."

Nanea handed a red Tootsie Pop to Lily. "Would you like to join the Honolulu Helpers?" Nanea asked Dixie.

"We're going to do all kinds of things for the war effort," Lily explained. "But we're going to have a lot of fun, too."

"Count me in!" Dixie said, racing ahead to the swings. Lily was right behind her.

Nanea followed. Tutu Kane was right. Dixie did have her own story. A sad one. Nanea wondered if there was anything she could do to make it happier.

New Tricks

anea was almost home when she saw
Mr. Cruz, the postman, at her mailbox.
He waved an envelope in her direction.
"Mail for Miss Nanea Mitchell," he called.

Nanea ran as fast as she could with her gas mask
and book bag. "Oh, thank you!" A letter from Donna.
Finally! Nanea plopped right down on the porch as
Mele bounded around from the back of the house to
greet her. With Mele at her side, Nanea tore the letter
open and began to read.

> *Meow, Nanea,*
>
> *I'm writing this on the boat. Kind of funny to
> think we can send mail while we're at sea! It's our
> second day out, and this is nothing like the trip we
> took coming to Honolulu. There are no fancy dinners*

or movies or shuffleboard games on the deck. Last night, we had a lifeboat drill at one in the morning! I heard some sailor say it was because there were submarines in the area. Mom says not to listen to idle chatter. But wouldn't a sailor know about things like that? I can't wait to reach San Francisco.

Please say hello to Miss Smith and everyone at school. I miss you something awful.

Kittens forever,

Donna

Nanea read the letter a second time, then folded it back into the envelope. Here she'd thought Donna's trip to San Francisco would be so glamorous. Nanea wrapped her arm around Mele, breathing Mele's good doggy smell. "Poor Donna. That sounded scary." She gave Mele a squeeze and then stood up. "Let's go answer her right now."

Nanea grabbed a couple of cookies from the kitchen and then went to her room and got out paper and a pencil. "How about some music while we write?" she asked. Mele wagged her tail.

There had been a lot of sadness that day with

Dixie's story and Donna's letter. "We need something cheerful, I think." Nanea moved a bag of Mary Lou's yarn and put on the recording of "My Little Grass Shack." She sat down on the bed, humming as she picked up her pencil. *February 9, 1942. Dear Donna*, Nanea started, but Mele's scampering caught her eye. She seemed to be bouncing back and forth to the music.

Nanea put down the pencil. "Can you twirl?" she asked, standing up and moving her hand in a circle. Mele cocked her head, watching Nanea's hand. "Oh, I know!" Nanea broke off a tiny bit of cookie and held it as she made a clockwise circle in the air. Mele lifted her nose, following the circle. "Good girl!" Nanea fed Mele the cookie. "Can you go the other way?" She got another chunk of cookie and moved her hand counterclockwise. Mele turned the other way and was rewarded again.

"You're getting the hang of this," Nanea said. She circled her hand clockwise and counterclockwise. Every time Mele turned in the proper direction, she got a cookie treat. "You are one smart dog," Nanea said, feeding Mele the last crumb. She brushed her hands, and then gave Mele a big hug. "I better get to work on this letter if I want to finish it before dinner." She sat back down and began to write.

> *I hope you are safe and sound in San Francisco. Your trip to California sounds awful. But I have news that should help you feel better. My mom has invited your dad to dinner every Thursday. We will treat him like family—except he won't have to do the dishes.*

Mele nudged at Nanea's hand, making her smudge the next word. "Mele, what are you doing?" Nanea looked at her dog. "The cookies are all gone." Mele turned in another circle. "Do you still want to dance?" Mele pawed at Nanea's leg. "Okay. Okay. Let me finish this."

> *You aren't going to believe this, but Mele keeps interrupting me. She wants to dance! I know it sounds crazy, but I've already taught her to twirl in both directions.*

Mele pawed at Nanea again. "All right!" Nanea put

her pencil down. "Let's take it from the top."

By the time Mom called Nanea to the kitchen to set the table, Mele had done so much twirling that she was ready for a nap. She curled up on Nanea's pillow and went to sleep.

At dinner, the house was as noisy as a mynah bird convention. Everyone was glad that Papa was home, and everyone was talking at once. Nanea was trying to tell her family about Donna's letter when David interrupted her. "Can you pass the rice, please?" he asked.

"That's your third helping." Nanea held the rice bowl away from him.

"I'm starved, Monkey!" David pretended to grab her plate of food.

"I guess you are." Papa chuckled at David's antics. "Hard day?"

David nodded as Nanea handed him the rice. He took a heaping spoonful. "Lieutenant Gregory invited me to help the Army Corps of Engineers." Lieutenant Gregory was the Army officer David worked for, and David talked about him all the time. He said that

Lieutenant Gregory was strict, but fair. "Like Pop."

David chewed and swallowed before he started talking again. "The engineers were digging trenches over by Kawai'ahao Church. Even though he didn't have to, Lieutenant Gregory picked up a shovel and pitched in with the rest of us." David paused. "He makes me want to do my best. To do even more."

"He sounds like quite a leader," Papa said.

David picked up his knife and cut into his chicken. "Lieutenant Gregory even let Gene come along." Gene was Lily's older brother and one of David's good friends. "He treated Gene like everyone else. He ended up hiring him," David added with admiration, "despite what happened."

"What do you mean?" Nanea asked.

"Gene went to enlist in the Army, and they turned him away," Mary Lou replied.

"They did?" Nanea asked. Gene was big and strong, like David. Why would he be turned away?

David frowned. "'No men of Japanese descent welcome,' they told him."

"I am sorry to hear that. Gene is a fine young man. He's as loyal and trustworthy as his father." Papa shook his head. "They've had it hard, what with Fudge spending so much time looking for work after his *sampan* was confiscated."

Fudge was Gene's and Lily's father. Nanea called him Uncle Fudge. It was hard for her to believe that anyone wouldn't trust him or the other Japanese people in Hawaii. But the Army had taken all the Japanese sampan fishing boats after the bombing of Pearl Harbor. They were worried that if enemy submarines returned to Hawaii, the Japanese fishermen on the islands would use their boats to bring spies ashore.

"I tried to get Fudge a job at the shipyard," Papa continued. "But I was also told, 'no Japanese allowed.'"

"It's a good thing Mrs. Lin gave him a job in her shop," Mom added.

"I can't wait until I'm old enough to join the Army," David said. "Then I'll enlist for Gene. That way at least someone from our 'ohana is serving."

Nanea knew that David thought of Gene and Lily and all the Sudas as part of their family, just as she did. But she hated hearing him talk about enlisting. She pushed her green beans around on her plate.

"Anyway," David said. "Gene and I are going back

tomorrow to finish digging the shelter."

"What about your schoolwork?" Mom asked, pressing her lips together.

David set down his fork. "Mom, what does math matter when there's a war on?"

"Education always matters," Mom said.

"I just want to do something," David said. "Something more than running messages."

Mom's coffee cup rattled in the saucer. "You're not eighteen."

"I will be in four months." David ran his hands through his dark hair. Beautiful hair that Uncle Sam would shave off if he went into the Army.

"I'm proud of you for being such a good friend to Gene," Papa said. "But your mother's right. We've got time before we need to talk about this."

Mom folded up her napkin. "Who's ready for dessert?" she asked.

No one said much as they ate their coconut pudding. Nanea and Mary Lou washed the dishes without their usual conversation. Then it was time to get ready for the blackout.

After two months, Nanea was almost getting used

to the pitch-black nights with the dark curtains drawn tight so no light escaped. She'd made a small lantern, and most nights she took it into her closet, where she'd curl up on a pile of pillows and read. But tonight Nanea didn't ask Mom to light her lantern. She didn't even bother to take a book into her closet. She just lay on the pillows, thinking. Even though she was perfectly still, Nanea felt like a tiny pebble being tumbled in the huge waves of her brother's words. *He's going to enlist when he's old enough,* Nanea thought. *And there's no way I can stop him.*

DOGS FOR DEFENSE

More than a week passed and David didn't say anything else about enlisting. Nanea went to school and did her homework and practiced for the next USO show. The Honolulu Helpers had their first meeting, and Auntie Rose helped them make red neck scarves. Then they made valentine cards for the soldiers. Nanea worked at Pono's Market, and she and Lily and Dixie collected bottles together.

Even though she tried to forget about David, Nanea's worry about him was winding itself into a bigger and bigger knot in her stomach, like one of Mary Lou's balls of yarn. Nanea hadn't been able to stop Donna from leaving. She didn't have much hope of stopping David from leaving either.

"Nanea!" Lily whispered to her at school. "Pay attention! It's time for the pledge."

Nanea stood up, placing her hand over her heart. As
she recited the Pledge of Allegiance with her class, she
stared at the date written on the blackboard. February
nineteenth. Less than four months until David's birthday. Mom always said, "Let's not borrow trouble," but
it was hard to take that advice. Nanea was distracted
during current events as Flora Bradley talked about
building model planes and being an aircraft spotter.

The minute Flora finished speaking, Albert waved
his hand.

"I'm delighted you want to go next, Albert." Miss
Smith motioned him to come up front.

Albert rarely shared anything, but today he stood
as proud and brave as King Kamehameha. "My current
event is about my dog, Tarzan," Albert began.

A couple of the kids snickered.

"It's a good name," he protested.

Miss Smith cleared her throat. "Scholars, let's give
the speaker our complete and courteous attention."

Albert straightened his shoulders. "Yeah. So Tarzan
and me—"

"Tarzan and I," Miss Smith corrected.

"Tarzan and I got invited to go through some tests

over the weekend. Uncle Sam is looking for dogs to help in the war. Any kind of dog." He jabbed his thumb at Teddy Fan. "Even a mutt like yours. They train them to be patrol dogs and messengers and even how to track enemy soldiers."

"Nifty!" Teddy exclaimed.

Nanea ran her finger around and around the hole in her desk where bottles of ink used to sit in the olden days. That didn't sound nifty. Dogs belonged with their families!

"And Tarzan did such a good job that the guy in charge said, 'Welcome to the Army.'"

Billy's hand shot in the air. "You enlisted?"

"Naw. Tarzan did." Albert stuck his hands in his pockets. "I'll miss him, but it's important that he's help-ing, right?"

"We're very proud of your contribution to the war effort, Albert." Miss Smith turned a warm smile in his direction.

"Well, the Army needs more dogs, but they won't find any as smart as Tarzan, that's for sure."

The room felt very hot all of a sudden. Nanea wiped her forehead.

"Tarzan sounds like a fine dog," Miss Smith said. "Thank you, Albert."

Albert sat down, and the class buzzed about Tarzan joining the Army. Nanea fanned her face. She'd been miserable the whole time Mele was missing after the Pearl Harbor attack. It was the worst two weeks of her life! If Mele joined the Army, she could be gone for months. Years! It was hard enough to think of David wanting to enlist! The thought of Mele leaving again was making Nanea dizzy.

"Are you okay?" Dixie asked. "Your face is all red."

"I just need some water," Nanea said. She raised her hand for permission to go out to the hall for a drink.

When Nanea returned to the classroom, she found paper and crayons on her desk. Miss Smith was starting read-aloud time. Nanea listened to the next chapter about the Ruggles family, but she didn't hear a thing. Instead, she covered her paper with doodles of dogs. Dogs with big brown eyes.

After school, Lily came to Nanea's house to plan their next Honolulu Helpers project. When they opened

the front door, the girls were hit with the aroma of cinnamon and ginger.

"I know that smell!" Lily exclaimed

"Elevator Lady spice cookies!" Nanea led the way to
the kitchen.

She loved the cookies almost as much as she loved
their name. Mom had gotten the recipe from a friend
in Seattle who had gotten the recipe from the lady who
ran the elevators at Frederick and Nelson department
store.

"Hello, girls." Mom set a plate of cookies on the
kitchen table. Mele hopped up on her hind legs, sniff-
ing. These cookies were her favorite, too.

"Hello, Aunt May," Lily answered.

"Thanks, Mom," Nanea said, taking a cookie. But
she didn't eat it. She looked at Mele, and all she could
think about was Albert giving up Tarzan. Mele stared
at Nanea as she set the cookie on a napkin.

"Nanea, I finished making your *holoku*. Would you
like to try it on?" Mom asked.

"I can't wait to see it," Lily said.

The girls and Mele followed Mom into the bedroom
Nanea shared with Mary Lou.

"It's beautiful!" Nanea exclaimed when she saw the dress on her bed. The fabric was a deep plum color printed with pink hibiscus, and the dress had a long skirt and wide ruffles at the neck and hem. Nanea had worn her sister's holoku, but this was the first one Mom had made just for her. Nanea couldn't wait to dance in the costume.

Nanea hugged her mom. "Thank you," she said.

"That train is so pretty," Lily said. "Kind of like a wedding dress. Model it for us!"

Nanea carefully unzipped the back. She knew to pull the dress over her head, and not to step into it, so that she wouldn't tear anything. Mom zipped it up and adjusted the fabric at Nanea's shoulders.

"You look so grown up," Lily said.

Mele barked in agreement, and the girls laughed. Nanea twirled in a slow circle, feeling the weight of the train sweep the floor. "Can I put on a record?" Lily asked, going over to the phonograph player next to Mary Lou's bed.

"Sure," Nanea answered. "But I should take this off so I don't get it dirty."

"That's very grown-up thinking," Mom

complimented her. She helped Nanea out of the holoku and then hung it up while Nanea changed into play clothes. "I'll be in the kitchen if you girls need anything," Mom said as she left the room.

Lily placed a record onto the player and lowered the needle. The girls began dancing *lele* steps forward and back.

"Hey, look at Mele!" Lily exclaimed. Mele was moving forward and back with the girls, almost in time to the music. "She's dancing, too."

"Good dog," Nanea said. She took the cookie off the napkin and broke off a tiny bit. "Forward and back," she said. Mele followed her hand and was rewarded with the sweet treat.

Lily laughed. "That's amazing." Nanea did an *'ami*, swaying her hips. Mele swayed, too.

"When did this start?" Lily asked.

"Last week." Nanea broke off another chunk of cookie for Mele. "It started with turns, and now she wants to do everything I do! So I've been teaching her."

Lily looked surprised. "Well, you're a good teacher, and Mele is one smart dog. Albert was bragging about Tarzan, but this is just as neat as helping Uncle Sam."

Nanea's light mood grew heavy at Lily's words. She took the needle off the record and hugged Mele close. "I know Mele's as smart as Tarzan," she admitted. "But I don't see how I could ever give her up. Not after already losing her once." She sat on the floor, with Mele in her lap.

Lily sat next to them. "That would be hard," Lily agreed.

"And there's something else." Nanea told Lily what David had said about enlisting. "I'm worried that he will join up, like those other boys at school."

Lily sighed. "He can't enlist yet, right?"

"Right," Nanea said halfheartedly.

Lily wrapped her arm around Nanea's shoulder and gave a squeeze. "Nobody knows what will happen between now and June."

Nanea nodded. But she wished she *did* know what would happen to one dancing dog and one brave big brother.

On the last Friday of February, when she got home from school, Nanea found a second letter from Donna in her mailbox. She ran to her room, Mele right behind her, and tore it open.

> *Meow, Nanea,*
>
> *We are finally settled in. My aunt and uncle fixed up an attic room in their house just for me. It's got blue checked curtains and a blue chenille bedspread. They remembered my favorite color, which was so very kind of them. But I'm having a hard time sleeping with city noise rather than geckos and mynah birds. Also, I keep expecting Dad to walk in the door any minute. I want us to be a family again. Mom says we have to be brave. But sometimes I can't help crying. The kids at my new school seem nice, but I miss you and Lily so much. Every night I wish on the first star I see that the war will end soon and the Three Kittens can be back together.*
>
> *Your friend,*
> *Donna*

Mele sniffed the letter in Nanea's hands. "Oh, she sounds so sad," Nanea said. Donna's letter felt like another brick on Nanea's wall of worries. Mele. David.

Donna. Nanea felt like curling up on her bed and having a good cry. Instead, she put on "My Little Grass Shack"—Mele's favorite—and they danced, telling the familiar story of longing for home. Mele licked her lips when Nanea sang the line about fish and *poi*.

When the song ended, Nanea felt lighter. Despite her worries, dancing with Mele had brightened her spirits. *The Army can have Dogs for Defense,* Nanea thought. *I have a dog that can dance!*

EXPLOSIONS IN THE NIGHT

🐚 CHAPTER 8 🐚

n the early hours of March fourth, a bad
dream about David falling into a very deep
hole caused Nanea to stir. Then she heard
boom-boom-boom!

Mary Lou jumped out of bed. "What was that?" The
bedroom windows rattled.

"Is it another attack?" Nanea's legs barely held
her as she got up and felt her way across the room in
the dark. Just three days earlier there'd been an air
raid drill. There had been many since December seventh. But Nanea knew this wasn't a drill. Not with
explosions!

"To the shelter," Papa called. Nanea was so grateful
he was working the day shift for a while so that he was
home in the middle of the night. She couldn't imagine
getting through this without him.

Nanea grabbed Mele. "Where's David?"

"Here!" In the darkness, Nanea could hear her brother hopping in the hall, trying to pull on his dungarees and run at the same time. "Did anyone hear the air raid siren?"

"No, but let's not take any chances," Mom said.

Papa ushered them all out to the pitch-black yard. Nanea couldn't see any stars in the cloudy sky. That made her feel even more frightened.

Once in their air raid shelter, Papa lit a small lamp.

"I heard three booms." Nanea pulled a whimpering Mele onto her lap.

"Me, too." Mary Lou grabbed Nanea's hand.

Nanea listened hard, waiting for another explosion. Mele quivered in her arms. "You poor baby," Nanea murmured. "I know you don't like it in here. I don't, either." This dark place had to remind Mele of the hole she'd been stuck in after the Pearl Harbor bombings. "I won't let anything happen to you," she promised.

Heart pounding, Nanea leaned against her mother. She stroked Mele's head as Mom pulled her close. Nanea couldn't stop the questions from going through her mind. *What had been bombed? Was anyone hurt? When was this horrible war going to be over?*

"Does anyone hear planes?" Mary Lou asked.

"Nope," David said. "And I don't hear any fire truck or ambulance sirens, either," he added. "So it doesn't sound like anyone's been hurt."

Nanea hoped David was right.

Just then the all-clear sirens clamored through the night, signaling that it was safe to leave the shelter.

Papa picked up Nanea and Mele and carried them into the house. "Try to get some sleep," he said as he tucked Nanea into bed. She heard the rattle of David's jalopy engine. "Where's David going?" she asked.

Papa smoothed the blanket over her. "To see if he can be of any help to Lieutenant Gregory. If there were bombs, there's bound to be cleanup."

"But won't David get arrested for being out after curfew?" Nanea asked.

"He has a pass," Papa assured Nanea. He bent to kiss her forehead. "Don't you worry. Your brother can take very good care of himself."

After Papa left, Nanea patted her pillow. Mele climbed up and slept next to her. But that didn't calm Nanea's worries. She wished David had never gone to work for Lieutenant Gregory. Then her brother would be home in his bed. Safe and sound. Nanea tossed and turned, thinking she'd never fall asleep, but she was so worn out, she finally did.

Nanea woke to the smell of Portuguese sausage. She pattered to the kitchen table with Mele at her heels.

"Good morning, Sunshine," Papa said.

Nanea yawned. "Do we know what happened last night?"

Mary Lou shook her head. "Not yet." There were dark circles under her eyes.

"There should be more news soon, on the radio," Papa added.

Nanea took a sip of juice. "Is David back yet?"

"He's still with Lieutenant Gregory," Mary Lou said, salting her eggs.

Mom clattered pans in the sink.

At that moment, David burst through the front door. "Well, they missed this time," he exclaimed.

"What are you talking about?" Mary Lou asked.

Mom handed David a cup of coffee and then sat

down next to Nanea at the table.

David buttered a Saloon pilot cracker and dropped it in his coffee cup. That was the way Tutu Kane drank coffee, and David did, too. "We found three craters near Roosevelt High School, on the side of Mount Tantalus." David took a sip of coffee. "Ah, this tastes good."

"Any damage?" Papa asked.

"At the school. Some shattered windows." David took another swallow. "On the mountainside, there are a bunch of broken trees and one big bomb crater."

"Does the Army know what happened?" Mary Lou asked.

"It looks like there were two planes, with two bombs each. Remember how cloudy it was last night? Lieutenant Gregory says they had to drop their bombs blind. They missed any important targets, so there was no real harm done."

Nanea pushed the fried egg around on her plate. "Will they come back?"

"Not likely, Monkey," David said confidently. "Lieutenant Gregory called it a nuisance raid. He said the Japanese came back to cause trouble but that Pearl Harbor's not likely to be worth their effort anymore."

Papa's job was at Pearl Harbor. Donna's father's, too. *Are they in danger every time they go to work?* she wondered.

Mom scraped her chair back. "I'm going to listen to the radio," she said, walking into the living room.

"Why were we worth the effort the first time?" Nanea asked.

"It's complicated," said Papa.

"I'm not a baby," Nanea said crossly. She knew her parents wanted to protect her, but sometimes not knowing was worse than knowing. "I can understand things, even if they're complicated."

David looked at Papa, and Papa nodded.

"You're right, Monkey," David said. "You are old enough to understand." David pulled out a chair and sat down. "Before the December attack, we had all our ships and planes in one place, Pearl Harbor, like this." David arranged the jam jar, salt and pepper shakers, and sugar bowl in the center of the table. "The Japanese attacked us there to destroy America's fleet and our ability to fight back." Then David pushed the dishes apart. "Now we've separated the ships and planes. That means Oahu's no longer such a valuable target to the

Japanese. It's a whole different ball game."

Mom called from the living room. "The radio says school's on today."

"Oh, good!" said Mary Lou. "There's a sock hop at lunch."

"That must mean there's nothing to worry about." Papa's voice was strong and calm.

Nanea wanted to believe him, but worry still clung to her like a sticky vine.

No Laughing Matter

'm going to faint!" Dixie shouted.

Lily studied the book she was holding. "It says here in the Junior Red Cross Handbook that you're not supposed to let the patient look at her own injury." She held the book out to Nanea.

"I'm trying to keep her from looking," Nanea said, brushing her hair back from her face in exasperation. The Honolulu Helpers were at the Red Cross for first-aid training, but it was not going well.

"I'm wounded, oh gadzooks, I'm wounded," Dixie declared, throwing an arm across her forehead.

Mrs. Sroat from the Red Cross frowned over at the girls. Nanea was doing her best to wrap Dixie's pretend wound the way Mrs. Sroat had instructed, but Dixie was squirming.

"Give me another bandage, please!" Nanea said to Lily. Then she turned to Dixie. "Be serious, will you?"

"Sorry." Dixie tugged at her red kerchief. "I was just trying to make it fun."

"But this is important," Nanea said sternly. "We are trying to earn our first-aid certificates."

Lily handed a length of white gauze to Nanea. Nanea looked over at Judy, who had created a complicated crisscross wrap on Alani's hand. Nanea tried to copy what Judy had done.

"This can't be right," Nanea said. Her wrap looked like a gigantic cocoon.

Mrs. Sroat inspected Nanea's work. "There is a great deal of silliness in this corner of the room," Mrs. Sroat said. "Try again."

Nanea did try again, this time on Lily, who was a much calmer patient. It helped that she didn't wiggle and giggle as much as Dixie, but Nanea was still having a hard time getting the bandage right.

Nanea's mother appeared. She had been teaching first-aid classes at the Red Cross for months. When she saw the bandage on Lily's hand, she rolled up her sleeves. "Let's not give up yet," she said.

Half an hour later, Nanea, Dixie, and Lily had all mastered the basic bandages. "Here are your first-aid certificates," Mrs. Sroat said. She shook her head at the girls. "I wasn't sure about you three, but you managed to work together after all. Well done."

Later that afternoon, Lily and Dixie came over to Nanea's house. They were staying for supper. It was Thursday, so Donna's dad would be there, and Dixie's dad was coming, too. So was Lieutenant Gregory. "The more the merrier," Mom had said.

A pan sat cooling on the counter. Dixie sniffed appreciatively. "Pineapple upside-down cake!" she exclaimed. "My aunt doesn't do much baking."

"It sounds like she has quite a houseful to cook for," Mom said, trimming the ends from some green beans. "You girls can go play now. I'll call you later to set the table."

When Nanea, Lily, and Dixie stepped into Nanea's bedroom, Dixie stopped. "Wow. You only have to share a room with one other person." She sighed. "You're so lucky."

"I guess I am," Nanea admitted.

"Trust me." Dixie nodded her head. "You are."

"Does Mele have any new tricks?" Lily asked.

"Tricks?" Dixie asked.

"Wait until I show you!" Nanea put a record of "My Little Grass Shack" on the player. Then she opened a dresser drawer, pulled out a package wrapped in wax paper, and removed a cookie. "Watch!"

As the music played, Nanea performed a kaholo right, with her right thumb up as if she was hitching a ride. Then she stepped kaholo left. Mele followed her from side to side. Nanea broke off a piece of cookie, and at the sight of the treat, Mele began to turn circles.

"Oh my gosh!" Dixie cried. "Mele is dancing!"

Nanea smiled. When the music ended, Nanea rewarded Mele with another bite of cookie and lots of praise.

"You taught her all those steps in the last week?" Lily asked.

Nanea nodded. "We've been working hard."

Dixie stroked Mele's head. "That dance is so cute. Have you shown anyone else yet?"

"No," Nanea said. "I'm planning to surprise David

with a performance at his birthday *luau* in June."

"I don't think you should wait that long," Dixie replied. "A hula dog is too cute to keep under wraps."

Before Nanea could answer, Mom called her to set the table and the girls rushed off, all humming "My Little Grass Shack."

"It's my favorite night of the week!" Mr. Hill announced when Nanea opened the door. Donna's dad said that every Thursday when he came for dinner.

Nanea introduced Mr. Hill to Dixie.

"My, you're a lucky girl to have friends like Nanea and Lily," Mr. Hill said. "They made my Donna feel right at home when we moved here."

Nanea blushed to remember she hadn't made Dixie feel at home right away. But Dixie just grinned.

"Have you talked to Donna lately?" Lily asked Mr. Hill.

"I called San Francisco long distance last night," he said. "Both my girls are doing well. Mrs. Hill got a part-time job with the *Chronicle* newspaper, and Donna is settling in at her new school."

Nanea thought that was perfect that Mrs. Hill was working for a newspaper. Mr. Hill loved reading newspapers!

"I sure miss them," Mr. Hill said, rubbing his chin. "The house is empty and lonely, and I can't finish any of my crossword puzzles without Donna's help." His smile was tinged with sadness.

Nanea wanted to say something to make Mr. Hill feel better, but she didn't know what words to use. She hated the war for separating families. And friends.

A few minutes later, Mr. Moreno and Lieutenant Gregory arrived at the same time. Dixie introduced her father to everyone, and then David introduced his guest, who was so tall, he looked like a coconut palm in a room full of bonsai trees. Lieutenant Gregory's close-cropped hair was strawberry blond, a shade less red than Papa's.

"I am so pleased to meet you both." Lieutenant Gregory shook hands with Mom and Papa. "And I'm grateful for this chance to tell you in person what a wonderful young man David is."

Papa smiled, and his chest puffed up like rising dough.

"We are very proud of him," Mom said. "Proud of all of our children." She wrapped an arm around each of her daughters.

"You must be Mary Lou." Lieutenant Gregory tipped his hat. Then he turned to Nanea. "And Monkey," he said. "I've heard all about you."

Nanea wanted to hide. Did the lieutenant really think her name was Monkey? "It's nice to meet you," she replied politely.

"Dinner will be ready soon," Mom said. "Please, go relax for a bit on the lanai."

Mary Lou served the men icy bottles of Kist soda as they made themselves comfortable on the back porch. Mr. Hill and Mr. Moreno were engaged in lively conversation, while Papa and David talked with Lieutenant Gregory. Mary Lou sat down and started knitting, but Nanea could see her sneaking looks at Lieutenant Gregory.

"Monkey?" Dixie asked as she helped Nanea fill the water glasses.

"It's David's nickname for me," Nanea said.

"Nanea," Mom said. "Please tell the men to come in to dinner."

When everyone was gathered at the table, Mele settled under Nanea's feet. She was on her best behavior and didn't beg for food. Nanea rewarded her with several green beans when Mom wasn't looking.

"Minneapolis must be so interesting," Mary Lou said to Lieutenant Gregory.

"Michigan, right?" Dixie inserted. They'd been learning major cities of the United States in class.

"Minnesota," whispered Nanea.

"Minnesota!" Dixie corrected her guess.

"Minnesota's home," Lieutenant Gregory admitted. "But for beauty, it's hard to beat Oahu." He nodded toward the centerpiece. "We have bluebells and asters, not lovely tropical flowers like those."

As they ate, the conversation turned to the bombings that had happened the day before.

"I'm betting that's the last time the Japanese waste their time and bombs on us," Mr. Moreno said. "They've got bigger fish to fry in the Pacific."

"It was rough to learn the Japanese just captured Singapore," Mr. Hill added.

"And those recent attacks in Australia." Papa shook his head.

"We need a break in the Pacific," David added.

Lieutenant Gregory nodded. "I know we can turn things around. Maybe at Midway."

That very morning at school, Miss Smith had pointed out the Midway Islands on the map. They were halfway between North America and Asia, which is how they got their name.

"How about some more chicken, Lieutenant Gregory?" Mom asked. "Mr. Moreno?"

The other guests all took seconds, except Dixie, who announced that she was saving room for pineapple upside-down cake.

Papa laughed. "It's the best on the island," he said.

After dinner, the men went back out to the lanai while Mom made coffee and Mary Lou sliced the cake. Nanea, Dixie, and Lily washed the dishes. Nanea thought of last Thanksgiving, when she and Donna and Lily had been in this kitchen together, laughing and talking as they cleaned up. That memory felt like it belonged to a different lifetime.

"Don't you think Lieutenant Gregory's handsome?" Mary Lou asked, placing a piece of cake on a plate.

"He reminds me of a movie star," Dixie said.

"Maybe John Wayne?"

Lily rubbed the tea towel over the plate. "He's not as handsome as David!"

"I bet he's a good dancer," Mary Lou added.

Nanea made a face. "What makes you say that?" She looked over at Lily, who rolled her eyes.

Mary Lou sighed dreamily. "He's so tall."

"Tall doesn't make good dancers," Nanea observed.

"Is that a mosquito I hear buzzing?" Mary Lou asked, flapping her hand in Nanea's direction.

Nanea just shook her head with a laugh.

When the coffee was ready, Mom and Mary Lou carried the cups while Nanea, Lily, and Dixie carried the plates to the lanai. Nanea sat by David. Mele sat at Nanea's feet, staring at her cake and whimpering.

"Not now, Mele," Nanea whispered, embarrassed. Mele's manners had been so good all evening.

Nanea moved her cake out of Mele's view, but her dog knew it was still there. Mele got up and turned in a pretty circle, just like she'd done in Nanea's room when they'd been dancing. Nanea slipped her a tiny bit of cake, and Mele turned in the opposite direction.

"Well done," Lieutenant Gregory said, clapping for

the trick. "That is a very talented dog!"

"Nanea's been training her," Dixie announced.

All of Nanea's family members were impressed. "Wow, Monkey," David said. "When did you have time to do that?"

Nanea was a bit embarrassed by the attention. She was also disappointed. Now her surprise for David's birthday luau wouldn't be a surprise. "We've been working on it for a few weeks," she admitted.

"She just learned how to do that?" Lieutenant Gregory was clearly impressed. "What a smart dog! Have you heard about Dogs for Defense? They're borrowing family pets for Uncle Sam," he explained.

"Like Albert's dog, Tarzan," Dixie chimed in. She filled Lieutenant Gregory in on their classroom conversation.

"It's a very important program," Lieutenant Gregory said, setting down his coffee cup. "The Army needs smart dogs that can be trained quickly."

Nanea froze. Was Lieutenant Gregory asking her to give up Mele?

Lieutenant Gregory stood up. "This has been a lovely evening, folks." He shook Papa's hand. "Now I've got to beat that curfew."

"We all do," said Mr. Hill, shaking Mom's hand. "Thanks for everything, May."

Mr. Moreno patted his stomach. "So *'ono!* Thank you for including Dixie and me."

"Supper was delicious, Mrs. Mitchell," Dixie said, gathering her things. "I'll see you tomorrow," she told Nanea and Lily. Her father took her hand, and they followed Mr. Hill out the door.

"I better scoot, too!" Lily bounded down the front steps. "See ya!"

Nanea watched from the front porch as everyone left. Mele was at her side, right where Nanea always wanted her to be.

Air Raid!

 week later, Nanea and Mary Lou were
finishing the Saturday morning breakfast
dishes. Papa was working another double
shift, and Mom was at the Red Cross. David was in
the backyard, whistling as he worked in the Victory
Garden. The whole family had helped plant the garden,
but David spent the most time there, pulling weeds
and watching for bugs. Papa was so proud of David for
carrying on the Mitchell family farming tradition. He'd
snapped pictures of David at work in the garden and
sent them to Grandma and Grandpop in Oregon.

Mary Lou handed Nanea the last dish to dry. "Did
you hear about the Varsity Victory Volunteers group
Gene started with some of the other Japanese boys?"
Mary Lou asked. "The VVVs, as they're called, are
building roads and warehouses and whatever else

needs doing. Anything to help the war effort."

Nanea nodded. "Lily's family is still upset that the Army wouldn't allow Gene to enlist because he's Japanese," Nanea said. "None of the Sudas would ever do anything to help the enemy!"

Mary Lou let the water out of the sink. "You know that and I know that," she said, "but lots of people don't. The VVVs will show them. Iris and I and a bunch of our classmates are meeting this afternoon to make sandwiches for them." Mary Lou looked at the kitchen clock. "Are you ready for hula class? We need to leave soon."

Nanea hurried to her room and picked up her 'eke hula. She practiced a few 'ami steps, swaying her hips from side to side. Mele, who had been sleeping on Nanea's pillow, got up and started waggling back and forth. "You silly hula dog," Nanea said, heading for the bedroom door. "We'll do some more practicing tonight. Are you ready to go?" But Mele didn't follow. She backed up, lifted her muzzle, and howled.

"What's wrong?" In an instant Nanea knew the answer to her question.

Mele was howling at an air raid siren. *Oh no!*

"Nanea!" Mary Lou's voice was calm but firm. "Come here."

This was the first air raid drill Nanea had been through without Mom and Papa.

"Now!" Mary Lou called again.

Nanea grabbed Mele and ran.

David was at the back door. "Head for the shelter."

Nanea hurried across the lawn, past the Victory Garden, to the shelter's opening. Mele whined and pawed at her as they climbed inside.

"It's okay, it's okay," Nanea murmured, stroking Mele's head. But it didn't feel okay. It was hard to be brave without her parents. Nanea tried not to think about all the bugs crawling in the earth above her, ready to drop in her hair.

"You're taking good care of Mele." Mary Lou gave Nanea a squeeze.

Nanea held tight to Mele as the siren blared on and on and on. "Do you think Mom and Papa found a shelter?" she asked in a tiny voice.

"The folks are okay, Monkey." David patted her knee. "Lieutenant Gregory has made sure there are shelters all around town."

"But what if it's not a drill?" Nanea asked.

"If it wasn't, we'd have heard planes or something," Mary Lou said. "You know what Mom says. Let's not borrow trouble."

The three of them sat without talking. Nanea's heart raced as she clutched a shaking Mele in her lap. And even though David and Mary Lou were acting as if there was nothing to worry about, Nanea could tell that they were nervous, too. Finally, the all-clear alarm sounded. "See?" Mary Lou said. "Just a drill."

"Come on, Monkey." David held out his hand.

Nanea didn't need any encouragement to leave the smelly shelter. Once outside, she shook her head vigorously, in case there were any spiders. Mele shook, too.

"Let's go," Mary Lou said. "Even with the drill, Tutu will be waiting for us."

Nanea gathered her things and, with Mele at her heels, followed Mary Lou on wobbly legs. This had been a drill. But what about the next time? What if Lieutenant Gregory was wrong about the Japanese? Last week at dinner he'd said they wouldn't bother with Hawaii again. But what if they did come back?

This terrifying question crashed through Nanea's

thoughts like storm waves breaking on the shore. Shaken, she joined the other students outside Tutu's lanai. Some of the girls whispered about the drill, but many of them stood as Nanea did, silent and still. She drew in a deep breath waiting for Tutu's invitation.

"Makaukau?" Tutu's question was gentle, and when she opened her strong brown arms, it was as if she was creating a safe harbor for her dancers. Her grandmother's strength and grace calmed Nanea's racing heart. She inhaled deeply, her nose filling with the good scents of Tutu's nearby flower garden.

"Ae," the dancers replied. To her surprise, Nanea did feel ready. The peacefulness of the movements, the joy of the music, the discipline of the steps—each element of the dance put the air raid drill farther and farther away. She got swept up in the stories they were telling through their dances. Stories about lovely hula hands and hospitality and love. The more she danced, the smaller her worries got, until they were mere grains of sand.

"You girls are ready for the next USO show," Tutu announced after class was over. "I'm very proud of you for working so hard. You will help our soldiers take their minds off their worries for a while, and that is a beautiful gift. You are an honor to the dance. Be safe as you go home," she added.

The students gathered their things and left, and Mary Lou headed to Iris's house to make sandwiches. Nanea and Tutu normally went to Pono's Market on Saturday afternoons. But today David was going to help Tutu Kane in the store. Nanea was grateful to have some time with Tutu, just the two of them, without any place to go. "I could use a piece of coconut cake," Tutu said to Nanea. "How about you?"

"Yes, please." Tutu made the most delicious coconut cake!

"Coming right up!" Tutu winked.

"May I put another record on while you get it?" Nanea asked.

"Of course." Tutu went into the kitchen.

For the next USO show, Nanea's class was dancing to "Liliʻu E," a song written in honor of Queen Liliuokalani. Tutu had told the class that they must be very regal when they danced. Nanea wanted to perform it perfectly, so she decided to practice it again. She dropped the needle onto the record and focused on the steps and hand motions to tell the story of the queen.

As soon as Nanea began dancing, Mele jumped up from a shady spot on the lawn. She paced around Nanea, wagging her tail. Nanea made a motion to shoo her away, but Mele merely cocked her head. It seemed as if she was asking, *Why can't I dance, too?* The expression on her furry face was so sweet that Nanea had to laugh. She patted her thighs, and Mele raised up on her hind legs. Nanea grabbed her front paws and danced her this way and that. Then Nanea let go, and Mele trotted forward and back before doing a doggy twirl.

"What's this?" Tutu came back, carrying two plates. "A dancing dog?" she asked, wonderingly.

Nanea froze. Tutu had told her that this dance was regal. Would she think Nanea was being disrespectful? But when she saw the smile in Tutu's eyes, Nanea relaxed. "I've been teaching Mele how to hula."

"So I see," said Tutu, setting the plates on the coffee table. "It looks like Mele enjoys it. Have you enjoyed teaching her?"

Nanea sat down and picked up a fork. "It's been a lot of fun," she said, taking a bite of cake. "At first I didn't think I'd have time, but teaching Mele helped me get my mind off other things." Nanea's voice trailed off as she thought of her worries about more attacks, the fear that David would enlist, and the suspicion that Lieutenant Gregory wanted Mele for Dogs for Defense. "And I like thinking about the stories I'm telling with each dance. I think Mele likes them, too. Especially the ones that mention fishing."

At the sound of her favorite food, Mele whined. She stared at Nanea's plate. "Mele likes fish *and* coconut cake," Nanea giggled, breaking off a piece of cake and feeding it to Mele.

"I'm glad you're having fun," Tutu said, taking a bite of her own cake. "We *all* need some fun during these trying times."

Nanea heard the clatter of heels on the walk. Mom came scurrying around the corner of the house and onto the lanai. She threw her arms around Nanea.

"Oh, I am so sorry Papa and I weren't with you kids for the air raid drill." She gave Nanea a squeeze. "Were you okay?"

"We did what we were supposed to," Nanea said.

"That doesn't surprise me." Mom stroked Nanea's hair. "You've become so grown-up and responsible."

"You'd be amazed at the things Nanea's been doing," Tutu said. She looked over at Mele and then winked at Nanea.

Mom raised an eyebrow. "What have you been up to?" she asked.

"Just hula," said Nanea. She giggled as she and Tutu shared a secret smile. "Do you want some coconut cake?" she asked.

"I thought you'd never ask," said Mom.

ANOTHER CHANCE

CHAPTER 11

Nanea slid her dime over to Dixie and took the War Stamp in return.

"That's your sixth stamp," Dixie exclaimed. "I wish everyone bought a stamp every week." She sighed. "We're never going to earn that Minuteman flag. I'm a terrible War Stamps monitor."

"No, you're not," Nanea said. But she was concerned. Nanea knew everyone in their class wanted to earn a Minuteman flag in honor of the men who were fighting. Why weren't more kids buying stamps?

Dixie's head dropped to the tabletop. "One of my cousins wet the bed again last night, and her crying woke everyone up. I haven't had a good night's sleep since we moved here." She twisted her neck to look up at Nanea. "I'm so tired. And you're good with math. I need your help adding up this money." She pushed a handful of coins across the desk.

Nanea sorted out the pennies, dimes, and nickels. "There's one dollar and fifty cents here," she said. She'd been watching Tutu and Tutu Kane at Pono's Market as they counted out change. She wanted to be ready for her chance at running the cash register.

"So that means I sold twelve stamps today?" Dixie rubbed her eyes, yawning.

Nanea shook her head. "No. A dollar fifty equals ten times fifteen." She grabbed a piece of scrap paper and wrote the numbers down and handed it back to Dixie. "You sold fifteen stamps."

Dixie yawned and then grinned. "I need more sleep. Thank you for your help." Dixie closed the cash box and returned the War Stamps and money to the supply closet.

Nanea was glad she could help. But Dixie never seemed to be able to do what she said she was going to do. She'd promised to cut out construction paper shamrocks for the Honolulu Helpers' St. Patrick's Day party, but her little cousins got hold of the scissors and ruined the paper.

"It's so hard sharing a room with them," Dixie

had explained. In the end, Nanea had to huddle in her closet hideaway during the blackout, cutting out four-leaf clovers by the meager light of her Crisco can lantern.

Dixie and Nanea walked back to their desks. "Are you still going to come on Saturday?" Nanea asked. The Honolulu Helpers were serving refreshments at the USO show in a few days.

"I'll be there!" Dixie exclaimed. "I promise."

"And you'll bring two dozen cookies, right?" That's what all the Helpers had agreed to.

"Two dozen," Dixie said. She snapped off a salute. "Aye, aye, sir."

Nanea let out a quiet sigh. She wanted to believe Dixie, but she just wasn't sure.

That night after dinner, Nanea and Mom sat at the kitchen table together. Mom drank coffee and planned her next Red Cross training meeting. Nanea made a to-do list for Saturday night's USO show. She'd be busy performing, so it was up to the other Honolulu Helpers to set up the refreshments. Half the girls were bringing

Kool-Aid, and half were bringing cookies. Nanea sighed, wondering if she should bake some cookies just in case Dixie didn't bring any.

"That was a heavy sigh," Mom said. She looked up from her own to-do list.

Nanea rubbed her writing hand. "How do you do it, Mom?" Since joining the Red Cross, Mom had taken charge of teaching first-aid classes and recruiting new members. "It's hard being responsible," she added.

Mom set down her pencil and reached over to pat Nanea's hand. "We're so proud of you for starting the Honolulu Helpers on top of everything else you're doing. But is it too much?" Mom's face looked concerned.

"No," Nanea shook her head. "At least it wouldn't be if people did what they said they would do." She sighed again. "People who are supposed to be my friend. Like Dixie."

"Oh." Mom raised her eyebrows. "What's up?"

Nanea picked up her pencil and twirled it in her fingers. "She wants to help, I know she does. But every time she says she'll do something, she doesn't. I'm probably going to have to bake her cookies for the USO show." Nanea looked straight at Mom. "Now I'm sorry I asked her to join the Helpers."

"I don't know Dixie very well yet," Mom started. "But she seems to have a good heart. I'm guessing she feels bad about letting you down. Can you give her another chance?" Mom smiled.

Nanea told Mom that Dixie shared a bedroom with her three young cousins and that she wasn't getting a lot of sleep. "She had her own bedroom back on Maui, at her tutu's house."

"That explains a lot," Mom agreed. "And I would imagine she also misses her tutu."

Nanea tried to imagine having to move away from her grandparents. Without Tutu, how would she learn hula stories? Without Tutu Kane, how would she learn about the birds and flowers of the island? But Nanea knew that Dixie missed more than her tutu.

"There's something else," Nanea said. Dixie had been so matter-of-fact about her mom leaving her to become an actress. But sitting here talking with her own mom made Nanea realize how hard it must be for Dixie. "Mrs. Moreno lives in California," Nanea said. She told Mom what Dixie had shared.

"Oh, I can't imagine being so far from my children." Mom shook her head sadly.

"Do you think it means she doesn't love Dixie anymore?" Nanea asked.

"Not at all." Mom leaned closer to Nanea. "Nothing ever changes a mother's love for her child." She paused to look Nanea in the eyes. "Nothing." Mom sighed. "Moving away must have been a tough decision for Dixie's mom to make."

"I wouldn't ever want you to go away," Nanea said.

Mom smiled. "That is something you *never* have to worry about." Then her smile faded. "But this part of Dixie's story tells me that you need to be even more patient with her. Show her lots of aloha."

Nanea nodded. Until that moment, she hadn't stopped to think about everything Dixie was missing.

"I'll give her another chance," Nanea promised.

Mom smiled. "That's the best we can do for a friend."

The Honolulu Helpers looked like a flock of small white and red birds as they flitted to and fro around

the USO hall in their uniforms. Nanea handed Lily the
task list. "You're the captain today," she said.

"Aye, aye!" Lily replied. She rounded up the Helpers
and began to assign jobs.

As Nanea turned away, she noticed Dixie running
into the hall, her neck kerchief askew. She was late,
but she was carrying a plate of cookies. Nanea smiled
and waved to her friend and then got back to her own
job of helping the littlest dancers prepare for their
performance.

"Do you see an extra lei anywhere?" Makana called
over to Nanea. Makana was holding the hand of one of
the littles, who looked about ready to burst into tears.

Nanea quickly searched the dressing room. A flash
of yellow caught her eye. "Here it is!" she announced.

The little girl sniffled as Nanea placed the paper lei
over her head. "Don't worry," Nanea whispered. "Just
have fun now, okay?"

The little girl walked away with a smile on her face.

Nanea felt a warm hand on her shoulder. "That was
kind of you," Tutu told her. "Maybe you will be a *kumu
hula* someday, too." Tutu smiled. "Now, you'd better get
dressed yourself."

With a light heart, Nanea hurried to where her costumes were hanging. Tonight she would wear her holoku for the very first time, as her class told the story of Princess Liliuokalani. But their first number was "My Little Grass Shack," so she put on her red hula top printed with small white flowers and the ti-leaf skirt she'd made with Tutu's instruction.

As the first notes of the song filled the USO hall, Nanea thought of Mele and how special it was telling that story of going home together. Nanea always smiled when she performed, but now she beamed thinking of her little dancing dog.

The sailors and soldiers clapped after every number. Nanea could see from their faces that Tutu was right. The hula stories were taking their minds off their worries.

When the program was finished, Nanea hurried to help serve refreshments. She filled a cup with Kool-Aid and handed it to the next man in line.

"You're not gonna make me wear that this time, are you?" a voice asked.

Nanea glanced up. "Tennessee!" she exclaimed. Then she blushed. The last time she'd served him punch, she'd spilled it all over his uniform, with a little help from Mele! "Don't worry. You're safe."

"Does that mean Mele isn't here?" he asked. "I was hoping to pet her."

"I'm sorry," Nanea said. "That other time was a mistake. She's not really allowed at the performances."

Tennessee looked disappointed. "It didn't seem like a mistake to me," he said. "Seeing that dog did me a world of good. But I can understand that hula and dogs don't exactly mix."

"How is your arm?" Nanea asked.

Tennessee tugged at the sling. "Another week or so and I'll be good as new," he answered. He finished the punch and handed the cup back to Nanea. "Thanks." Tennessee put his cap back on. "I best get going."

"He looked sort of sad," Dixie said as Tennessee walked away.

"It's too bad the dancing didn't cheer him up," Lily added.

"Maybe something else would," Nanea said. "Or *someone* else."

"What do you mean?" Dixie asked.

"Tennessee wanted to see Mele," Nanea explained.

"Imagine how happy he'd be if he saw her dancing!" Lily finished excitedly.

"Exactly!" Nanea said.

Dixie nodded her head. "What a great idea."

"What's a great idea?" Tutu asked. When Nanea explained, Tutu smiled. "That will really take the men's minds off their worries. In fact, I think you and Hula Dog should perform at the USO show next Saturday."

Nanea gulped. "The one at the Royal Hawaiian Hotel?" That was such a fancy place, and it was only a week away. Nanea was nervous, but then she thought of Tennessee. No matter what, she and Mele would be ready.

PRESENTING HULA DOG

🐚 CHAPTER 12 🐚

anea went through her 'eke hula for the third time, making sure she hadn't forgotten anything. *"Pu'ili?"* she asked.

"Check," Lily replied, touching the bamboo sticks.

"Kupe'e?" asked Nanea.

Dixie picked up the ankle decoration. "Check."

"What's this?" Lily picked up a piece of fabric that was on the floor.

"Mele's skirt!" Nanea exclaimed. "I almost forgot!"

Lily smiled. "I've never seen you so nervous."

Nanea sighed. "I *am* nervous. What if Mele forgets what I've taught her? What if we mess up?"

"You won't mess up," Dixie reassured her.

"And if you do, just keep dancing," Lily said.

"The show must go on!" Dixie added, flinging out her arms.

Her dramatics made Nanea laugh. "Okay. I'm ready. Let's go."

David drove Mele and the girls to the hotel. One of the bellmen ran over as they all walked inside. "David!" Darrell exclaimed. "You know dogs aren't allowed."

Mele wagged her tail as if to say she would forgive the hotel for that rule.

"She's in the show," David explained.

Darrell's forehead wrinkled under his cap. "But she's a dog!"

A man in a suit walked over. The gold name tag on his jacket read *Mr. DeSoto, Manager.* "Is there a problem?" he asked.

Nanea held her breath. She hadn't thought about Mele not being allowed in a hotel. What if they couldn't do the act?

Darrell pointed at Mele. "Dog trouble."

"I don't see any dogs." Mr. DeSoto smiled. "Just hula dancers here for the USO show." He winked at Nanea.

Darrell looked at Mele. He looked at Nanea. He looked at Mr. DeSoto. "Of course, all performers are welcome." He swept his hand in a wide gesture, and Mele trotted right in like she was used to such posh digs.

Nanea had gotten peeks into the Royal Hawaiian Hotel before when she had waited outside for David to finish working, but this was her first time inside the lobby. It was no longer being used as a hotel. The military had turned it into a place for R & R—rest and relaxation—for the servicemen. Before the war, guests had paid a lot of money to stay in the luxurious rooms. Now servicemen could stay for just a few dollars each night, enjoying the beach and free local entertainment.

"Look up there," Lily whispered as they crossed the large room.

The three girls tilted their heads back, admiring the enormous crystal chandeliers glittering overhead. Thick rugs covered the polished floors, and the elegant rattan chairs and sofas were dotted with plump color-ful pillows.

"This looks like a scene out of a movie," said Dixie.

The manager escorted them to the ballroom. A

double row of elegant columns carried Nanea's eye to a long bank of windows that framed blue sky and sunshine. There were rows and rows of chairs lined up like silent soldiers. Lots of people would be watching the debut of Hula Dog!

Tutu stood on the stage holding open the curtain. Nanea could see the other dancers behind the thick red drapes. "Nanea!" Tutu called out. "We're just getting ready to warm up."

"Wish us luck," Nanea said, twisting Mele's leash in her hand.

"Luck!" said Dixie. "But you won't need it."

"We'll be right up front," Lily added.

"Break a leg, Monkey," David said. "And I guess you should break a paw, Mele."

Tutu let the curtain fall closed behind Nanea. Mele sat in the wings, watching, while the dancers warmed up. Nanea could hear the chairs on the other side of the curtain squeak and scrape the floor as the arriving soldiers took their seats.

The lights dimmed to signal the start of the show. Nanea took several deep breaths to calm herself. But she was so preoccupied with the Hula Dog act that she got out of rhythm with her pu'ili as she danced to "Green Rose Hula." A stern look from Makana got her back on track. The song finished, and the girls bowed their heads. "You weren't paying attention," Makana whispered as they exited the stage.

"Sorry." Nanea shook her head to clear it of anything but dance steps. She squirmed out of her skirt and yellow performance top with its orange and red hibiscus, changing clothes as quickly as she could.

"Ready?" Mary Lou asked.

"I hope so." Nanea stroked Mele's head to calm herself.

Mary Lou signaled to Tutu to introduce the act. "This is my grandson, David Mitchell," Tutu announced. "He'll be playing ukulele for his sister, Nanea Mitchell."

Nanea walked to the center of the stage. She posed, waiting.

"And this afternoon Nanea is dancing with a new partner—Mele, the Hula Dog!"

David started "My Little Grass Shack," and Mele pranced out on the stage. There were lots of chuckles and some "awws" and "good dogs."

Nanea moved her feet and hands to David's music. Mele watched, wagging her tail.

The men in the audience chuckled a little louder. That made Nanea even more nervous. David played the first few measures again.

"Mele," she said. "Dance!"

Mele shook herself from head to toe. Then she cocked her head. Nanea did a kaholo right, made the hitchhiking motion with one thumb, while her other hand rested on her hip. Nanea folded her arms across her chest, and then drew an hourglass in the air with her hands.

As if that had been the cue she'd been waiting for, Mele stood on her hind legs. She pranced forward and back, side to side, turning in circles each time Nanea made a swaying motion. When David sang the last words of the song, Nanea brought her hands together, reaching them out over her pointed foot.

Soldiers and sailors jumped to their feet, cheering and stamping.

Afterward, the dancers served refreshments to the soldiers on a patio overlooking the ocean. Dixie and Lily rushed up to Nanea, who was pouring punch.

"You stole the show!" Dixie gushed.

Lily nodded. "Everyone is talking about Hula Dog!"

"And her talented teacher," David added, giving Nanea a thumbs-up.

"Your first solo. Almost," added Mary Lou, with a sisterly wink. "Good job."

"That was some number." Tennessee stood in front of Nanea, grinning.

"You gave me the idea," Nanea told him. "I hope seeing her did do you a world of good," she added, echoing Tennessee's words from the week before.

"Would the star mind if I said hello?" he asked. "As soon as I saw her onstage, I was hoping I could pet her."

Nanea was surprised at how eager Tennessee sounded. "Sure. Come on."

Mele was lapping at a bowl of water, and Tennessee fussed over her like she was Rin Tin Tin.

"Almost makes me feel like I'm back home with my Blue," Tennessee said. "Whoever said dogs are man's best friend said a mouthful. Gosh, I miss that mutt."

Soon a crowd had gathered. Tennessee reluctantly stepped away from Mele, giving some of the other men the chance to get close to her.

Nanea was surprised that some of those big strong men wiped tears from their eyes after petting Mele. Almost every one of them commented about a dog they'd left behind. It made Nanea happy and sad at the same time.

Tennessee hung around until the last soldier had left. "Thanks for letting me see her," he told Nanea. He gave Mele one last scratch behind the ears. "I best be pushing off, too," he finally said.

"Aloha," Nanea called after him. Then she knelt down and wrapped her arms around Mele's neck.

"Good dog," she said. "Good, good dog."

A Shot
in the Arm

O n the first day of April, Nanea pored over the newspaper as the family ate breakfast. She needed an article to take to school for current events.

"Did you see this?" Nanea pointed to a photograph of the Aloha Tower. She knew it had been painted in camouflage colors to hide it from enemy planes. But she didn't know about this latest change. "They've painted the clock face black!"

"On the *mauka*—the mountain side," David said. "I've seen it. Looks ugly."

"Sure does," Mary Lou agreed. "It makes me sad."

Mom set some fruit and toast in front of Nanea. "It makes me sad, too," she said. "But we don't want anything to happen to the tower."

"The military is doing its job," added Papa.

"That clock's a year older than I am," Mary Lou said. "Sweet sixteen."

"Yes. And it's like a friendly smile showing everyone who comes here about the aloha spirit," Nanea said. "Tutu says it's like the Golden Rule: It's important to treat everyone and everything as you would like to be treated."

Mom handed Nanea a plate of scrambled eggs and rice. "They can paint the clock black," she said, "but there's not enough paint in the world to cover up aloha spirit."

"That's true." Papa set down his fork. "Jay, one of the guys at the shipyard, lost his car in the attacks." He wiped his mouth with his napkin. "A couple of the machinists' wives have been sending along homemade doughnuts to sell at coffee breaks. They've already raised fifty dollars toward getting Jay a new car."

"And think about Iris's family," Mary Lou said. "Right after the bombing, they took in that lady— Trina—and her baby when her house and everything they owned was destroyed in the bombing." Mary Lou paused. "And her husband was on the USS *Arizona*," she added softly.

Nanea set the newspaper aside. When Pearl Harbor was attacked, so many men—thousands—had lost their lives on ships like the *Arizona*. Their families now had to go on without their loved ones. Trina's son would never know his father. Nanea couldn't imagine growing up without Papa. She blinked back tears.

"The aloha spirit means we share each other's joys and sorrows," Mom said softly. "No matter what."

Nanea nodded. In the spirit of aloha, she had given up her teddy bear when Iris was collecting toys and clothes for Trina's son. Holding on to that aloha spirit seemed to be helping everyone get through this war.

At school, Miss Smith called on Dixie to report on the War Stamps sales.

Dixie dragged her feet walking to the front of the room. "Thank you to everyone who's been buying stamps," she said. "But we're only at seventy-five percent participation. We need ninety percent for the flag."

Nanea glanced at their teacher. She usually was so proud of her students, but now she looked disappointed. From the murmuring in the classroom, Nanea could tell that her classmates were disappointed, too.

Before Dixie could finish her report, she was interrupted by a bell.

"It's time to report to the gymnasium," Miss Smith announced.

All the students groaned. Everyone on Oahu had to have certain vaccinations by order of the military governor. This was the day the Red Cross was at Lunalilo school to give shots.

In the gymnasium, Nanea, Dixie, and Lily waited together. "I can't watch!" Dixie ducked her head into Nanea's shoulder as Albert got vaccinated in each arm.

He winced, but he strutted away. "Piece of cake!"

"Just a pinch," the nurse said when it was Nanea's turn. "Here. And here. All done."

Nanea rubbed her arms. The shots felt like more than pinches. They hurt! But she hadn't even said ouch.

"You all did a fine job," Miss Smith said when they returned to the classroom. "I know it was difficult, but those shots will keep us all strong so that we can keep working toward winning the war."

Nanea looked at Dixie. Their stamp sale needed a shot in the arm, too.

After school, Nanea found something in her mailbox at home that eased the lingering ache from the shots. A letter from Donna! Nanea patted the spot next to her on the porch and Mele curled up there. Nanea began to read:

> *Meow, Nanea,*
>
> *Yesterday I went to school, and two of my new friends were gone. Their families have been sent away to a war relocation camp called Manzanar. It's happening to all the Japanese living on the West Coast, not just here. Susie and Emi were the first people to invite me to sit with them at lunch. At first I wanted this war over so the Three Kittens could be back together. Now I also want it over so Susie and Emi can come home.*
>
> *Your friend,*
> *Donna*

Nanea's hand dropped to her lap. "Oh, that's terrible," she said. She reached for Mele and pulled her close. It was bad enough when Uncle Fudge got sent away; he was a grown-up. What would it be like for kids? *Would they get to stay with their families?* Nanea wondered, rubbing her still-tender arms. The thought of them being separated caused Nanea more pain than a million shots ever could.

All Fired Up

'll be home late tonight," David called as he ran out the door. "Work!"

"I'll be home late, too," Mary Lou called, running after him. "I'm cooking for aid workers again over at the church."

"You forgot your lunches!" Mom chased after them.

"You're awfully quiet this morning, Sunshine," Papa said.

Nanea stirred raisins and cinnamon into her oatmeal. "I got a letter from Donna yesterday."

"Oh?" Papa said. "Is everything okay?"

Nanea stopped stirring. "She wrote about something that happened at her school. She said it's happening to Japanese people all over the West Coast." Nanea told Papa about Emi and Susie. "Why were they sent away?"

Papa scooted his chair away from the breakfast table, patting his knee. Nanea went to sit on it, leaning her head against Papa's chest. No matter how much Mom scrubbed, his work clothes always smelled of oil from the ships he worked on. But Nanea didn't mind it. It was part of Papa.

"I don't agree with it, but the Army has decided that for the safety of the country and the safety of Japanese Americans, it's best that they be moved," he said.

"But why?" Nanea asked.

"When you get to school today, look at the globe. You'll see that Japan is directly across the Pacific Ocean from the West Coast of the United States." Papa shrugged. "I guess the people in charge think if the Japanese military attacked that area, the people of Japanese descent living there might help them and fight against Uncle Sam."

"So it's like what the FBI thought about Uncle Fudge? That he wouldn't be loyal?" she asked.

"That's a big part of it," Papa said.

"No Japanese American I know would fight for the enemy," Nanea said.

"I agree," said Papa, "but I'm not in charge."

"Well, if I was in charge, I wouldn't make people leave their homes and schools," Nanea said. "I would believe in them."

Papa smiled. "I'm so proud of you." He patted her back. "You know better than to judge a book by its cover. You are really growing up. And I guess that makes sense, with a special birthday just around the corner. Now when is it again?" he teased.

"Papa! You know. It's next Saturday," Nanea said.

"That's right. My Sunshine turns ten on April eleventh." He winked. "I would never forget that. I'll see you after school." He kissed the top of her head. "Now it's good-night for me."

"I wonder where David is," Nanea said as she finished setting the dinner table.

"We may have to start without him." Mom took a steaming dish out of the oven.

Just then, the front door burst open and David hurried in with Lieutenant Gregory.

"Sorry we're late," David said. "Lieutenant Gregory was speaking to the Hawaii Defense Volunteers, and he invited me along." David nodded toward Lieutenant Gregory. "So I invited him to dinner."

Mary Lou quickly set another place at the table as Mele trotted over to say hello.

"There's that smart dog," Lieutenant Gregory said, giving Mele a pat.

Nanea tugged Mele away. "Leave the company alone," she told her dog.

"We're glad you're here," Mom said. "Dinner's ready."

Papa shook Lieutenant Gregory's hand. "Please. Sit down."

Mom and Mary Lou set bowls and plates on the table. Papa passed the platter of fish to Lieutenant Gregory.

"What did you talk to the volunteers about?" Papa asked.

"Their efforts, mostly," Lieutenant Gregory answered, serving himself. "I try to encourage people by letting them know that even small contributions help the war effort." He passed the platter back to Papa.

"He's a good speaker," David said. "He got people all fired up and eager to do more."

Lieutenant Gregory ducked his head modestly. "I just say what I believe."

"And you make others believe, too," David added with admiration.

Lieutenant Gregory smiled at Nanea when she passed him the bowl of rice. "How is school, Nanea? David tells me you like third grade."

"Nanea's a great student," David said proudly.

Nanea smiled at her brother. "Our class is trying to earn a Minuteman flag," she told Lieutenant Gregory.

"Admirable goal," Lieutenant Gregory nodded.

"But we're not doing very well," Nanea added.

"You need a pep talk from Lieutenant Gregory," David said with a laugh. "That would change things."

"Nanea's certainly been doing her part," Papa said. "She's bought a stamp every single week."

Lieutenant Gregory looked impressed. "Every dime adds up," he said.

"Our class is still trying to get to ninety percent participation," Nanea admitted. At first, she'd blamed Dixie. But Nanea knew that it was not just up to Dixie. The whole class needed to pitch in.

After dinner, Lieutenant Gregory excused himself

before dessert, explaining that he had to make a stop on his way back to the base. "I have to leave now if I'm going to make it back before curfew," he said. "It was a pleasure seeing all of you again. And you, too, Mele."

Mele left her place next to Nanea's chair to lean against Lieutenant Gregory's leg. Lieutenant Gregory reached down and scratched Mele's ear.

"She likes you," Mary Lou said.

"Next time I hope I'm here long enough to see her latest tricks," Lieutenant Gregory responded. "She's one smart dog."

Nanea patted her leg, motioning Mele to come back to her. *She's **my** smart dog*, thought Nanea. *Not Uncle Sam's.*

"I got another letter from Donna," Nanea said on the Wednesday before her birthday as she and Lily walked to school. She handed it to Lily.

> *Meow, Nanea,*
> *I'm so sad I'll miss your birthday this year. I sure hope I can celebrate with you next year.*

Here is something I'm not celebrating: Sugar is going to be rationed all over the country. That means no more bubble gum! I'm trying to make my supply last. And guess what? Our school is trying to earn a Minuteman flag, too. That makes me feel like we Three Kittens are doing something together.

Your friend,

Donna

"Oh, poor Donna," Lily exclaimed, handing the letter back to Nanea. "How will she survive without bubble gum?"

"I don't know," Nanea said. "We should send her some of her favorite foods, like mochi or Mom's guava bread," she suggested.

"When she comes back, we'll throw her a big luau— desserts only," Lily declared.

Nanea smiled. "That would be just the kind of luau Donna would love."

The mention of a party reminded her that David's birthday luau was coming up in less than two months. The luau to celebrate his eighteenth birthday. Nanea shivered. He would be old enough to enlist.

Dixie ran up to them as they entered the classroom. Nanea thought she'd be interested in the part about the Minuteman flag in Donna's letter, so she read it to her.

"Isn't that neat?" Nanea said. "Two schools separated by a huge ocean and we're both working for the same prize!" She put the letter back in her pocket.

"They'll probably win," Dixie said glumly, heading to her desk. "But we won't."

Nanea felt bad as she took her seat. She didn't mean to upset Dixie with Donna's letter. She thought Dixie would like the idea that both schools were working to support the war effort.

Miss Smith had just finished taking attendance when there was a knock at the classroom door. "This must be our special guest," Miss Smith said mysteriously.

When Miss Smith opened the door, Nanea nearly fell off her chair. It was Lieutenant Gregory!

Lieutenant Gregory saluted. "Reporting for duty, ma'am."

"A real soldier," Albert whispered loudly.

"He looks like the movie star, Gary Cooper," said Flora.

Nanea's classmates were abuzz to have a real live

officer in their very own classroom. Nanea was nervous. Was he here to talk about Dogs for Defense?

"First, I want to thank your teacher for allowing me to spend a few moments with you today." He nodded toward Miss Smith. "And I want to thank a young lady who is doing a very important job in your class: your War Stamps monitor, Miss Dixie Moreno."

Everyone turned to look at Dixie. Her cheeks were as pink as if she'd been tap dancing for an hour.

"Now, people think that I have an important job because I'm in the Army." He gave a little smile. "But do you know who has an even more important job?"

"No!" Billy Cruz blurted out.

Miss Smith put her fingers to her lips. "Raise your hands, please, scholars."

Lieutenant Gregory drew a big circle with his hand, encompassing every student in the class. "You. And your parents. You see, Uncle Sam can't win the war without you. And you know what matters most?"

Thirty-two heads shook no.

"I'll tell you. It's the little things. Like your mothers saving their cooking grease to help make ammunition. Or writing a letter to a wounded serviceman."

Lieutenant Gregory reached into his pocket and pulled out a dime. He held it up to the class. "Or bringing in one thin dime to buy a War Stamp." He put the coin back in his pocket. "Now, can Uncle Sam count on your help?" he asked.

"Yes, sir!" Billy shouted. This time Miss Smith didn't correct him.

"I think Billy speaks for the class, Lieutenant Gregory," Miss Smith said.

"That's the spirit." He saluted. "I know we'll win with students like you in the fight." He smiled at Nanea, nodded at Miss Smith, and left the room.

"Wow! A real soldier!" Albert exclaimed again.

"And he came here just to talk to us," said Flora. "Dixie, do you know him? He knows you!"

"I'm going to bring in *two* dimes next week," Billy announced.

It took Miss Smith a while to quiet the class and get to their spelling lesson.

David was right, Nanea thought. *Lieutenant Gregory's words do get people fired up. And it must have been David who asked Lieutenant Gregory to come talk to our class.*

Nanea looked at Dixie, who had a huge smile on her

face. *Imagine not being able to go home and tell your mom about something like this*, Nanea thought. *They're going to have a lot to catch up on whenever Dixie goes to California.*

As she numbered her paper to copy down the spelling words, Nanea felt a tap on her arm.

"*Mahalo*," Dixie whispered. "Thank you. This is the best day ever."

Nanea returned Dixie's smile. She had a feeling that on the next War Stamps day there would be so many dimes, it would be hard for Dixie to keep up.

A BIRTHDAY
MYSTERY

CHAPTER 15

Nanea rolled over. Something was different—
and it wasn't just that she was a year older.

Mary Lou was already up and her bed was
made. Odder still, there was a note safety-pinned to her
sister's pillowcase. Nanea blinked. Her name was on it.

Nanea pulled back her covers and hopped to the
floor, full of anticipation.

"Hey, Mele," she said. "Wake up!"

She opened the note. *Go see Auntie Rose for your first
birthday treat and your first clue.*

Nanea shook her head. What was going on? She
threw on her clothes. "Come on, Mele. Let's solve this
birthday mystery." She was going to be a detective, like
Nancy Drew!

Auntie Rose's front door opened before Nanea
could knock. "I thought it might be you. Happy

birthday!" Auntie Rose handed over a fragrant sack, along with another note. This one said: *Get cracking to your favorite seed shop.*

That was an easy clue. Nanea pulled a sugar-coated malasada out of the sack. "Thank you, Auntie!"

"Have fun!" Auntie Rose called as Nanea bit into the warm doughnut. She and Mele raced to Mrs. Lin's. Nanea wiped her sticky fingers on her shorts before going into the store. "Wait here," she told Mele.

"Is that Sherlock Holmes I see?" Mrs. Lin pretended to look at Nanea through a magnifying glass.

Nanea giggled. "It's me! Nanea, the detective."

"Ah, then." Mrs. Lin nodded. "I have a secret message for you, Nanea the detective." She handed over a packet of *li hing* cherry crack seed with a note taped to the back.

Nanea read the note aloud. *Go to the place where chocolate candy and a fragrant flower live together.* "This is a tricky one," she said.

"You can figure it out," Mrs. Lin encouraged.

Nanea scrunched up her face, thinking. "A florist shop?"

Mrs. Lin chuckled. "Not exactly."

"A candy store?" But that was a silly guess. Candy stores didn't sell flowers.

"Think about different kinds of candy and flowers," suggested Mrs. Lin.

"Well, there are candy bars, like Baby Ruths," Nanea said. "And *pikake* and ginger flowers are fragrant."

Mrs. Lin smiled.

"Am I getting warm?" Nanea asked.

"Warm*er*." Mrs. Lin straightened a display of dried plums.

Nanea thought hard. *What other kinds of chocolate candies were there? Chocolate-covered cherries, Tootsie Rolls, chocolate kisses, and*—"Fudge!" she cried. "Fudge is a chocolate candy, and Lily is a fragrant flower."

Mrs. Lin chuckled. "You are one sharp detective."

Nanea and Mele ran pell-mell to the Sudas' house. Lily opened the front door to Nanea's knock.

"You'll never guess," Nanea exclaimed. "Mary Lou made a treasure hunt, and it led me here!"

Lily wiggled her eyebrows. "Oh, I might be able to guess." She opened the door wider. In the living room, Nanea could see her entire 'ohana, including Uncle

Fudge and Aunt Betty and their boys, Auntie Rose, and even Dixie. "Surprise!" Lily cried. "Happy birthday."

Everyone crowded onto the front porch, kissing and hugging Nanea.

Mary Lou slipped a lei over Nanea's head. "Happy birthday, baby sis."

"We wanted to surprise you, Monkey," David said. "Did it work?"

Nanea sniffed the lei. "And how!"

"Now for the best part," Tutu said. "A picnic!"

"We've saved up our gas coupons so we get to drive!" Lily said.

Nanea, Lily, and Dixie grabbed hands and ran to squeeze into the backseat of Uncle Fudge's car with Mele, Tutu, and Aunt Betty. By the time the caravan pulled away from the curb, three vehicles were filled to the brim with people and picnic goodies.

"You should have seen your face!" Dixie giggled.

"Your eyes got like this!" Lily opened hers wide to demonstrate.

They drove to a stretch of Waikiki Beach by the aquarium. Even with the barbed wire, Nanea thought the beach was beautiful. After the cars were parked, everyone got out and grabbed something to carry.

"Look!" Nanea shifted the blankets in her arms to point toward Kapiolani Park. It was filled with junker cars spaced out evenly like pieces on a game board. "Why did they do that?" she asked.

"It looks terrible," added Dixie.

David explained. "It's part of the Army's plan to keep enemy airplanes from landing."

Nanea felt like she'd swallowed sand. Even on birthdays, there was some reminder of war.

"Don't worry, Monkey. It's only a precaution. No worries on this special day. I'll race you to the water!"

Mele barked and ran on the beach as all the kids splashed in the water. "Who's going to help fish for supper?" Papa called to them, pulling out the poles.

"Me!" Nanea hadn't thought of her favorite pastime in such a long time.

"I bet I catch the biggest one," David bragged.

"Nothing doing," said Gene. "That will be me."

They laughed good-naturedly when Lily reeled in the catch of the day.

While the fish cooked over the small fire Papa and Tutu Kane built, Nanea, Lily, Dixie, and Mary Lou held a sand castle–building contest with David, Gene, and Tommy. The boys won only because Mele got excited and knocked over the girls' castle.

"Anybody hungry?" Mom asked.

"Starved!" Nanea replied. Every single one of her favorite foods was on the menu.

"I made two-finger poi." Tutu winked at Nanea. "Just the way you like it."

Nanea scooped up a taste of the thick mashed *taro* with her index and middle fingers. "So 'ono."

Papa and Tutu Kane roasted frankfurters, and Nanea, Lily, and Dixie ate two each. They devoured watermelon and potato salad, but they made sure to leave room for cake.

David licked frosting from his fingers. "So what do you think, Monkey? Do you want any presents?"

"Of course she does," Tutu Kane said. "This is a special birthday." He shook his head. "Ten years old."

Mom produced a small stack of gifts for Nanea. Lily had made her a picture frame out of Popsicle sticks, like the one she'd made for Donna. Dixie presented her with a pair of red barrettes.

"I thought those would look pretty in your hair,"

Dixie said as Nanea unwrapped them.

"They will!" Mary Lou agreed.

David gave Nanea a new Nancy Drew mystery, and Mary Lou's gift was a coin purse with three kittens stitched on the front. Tutu had sewn matching pineapple-print skirts for Nanea and Mele. "A perfect fit!" Mom pronounced when Nanea tried hers on. Mele couldn't be caught to model hers. She was too busy chasing beach birds.

Next, Nanea unwrapped the package from her Mitchell grandparents. "A camera!" she exclaimed. "And film!"

"It's just like Donna's," Lily noted.

Nanea nodded. "I can't wait to try it out!"

The last gift was from Tutu Kane. Nanea gasped when she saw the shell lei. "Oh, thank you! *Mahalo ia 'oe.*" She fastened the string of tiny shells around her neck.

Years ago, Tutu Kane had gathered these shells from the island of *Ni'ihau.* He'd kept them until the right moment to make special leis for each of his grandchildren.

"It's beautiful." Nanea touched her neck gently,

knowing that it had taken her grandfather a long time to make such a lei. It was a treasure greater than diamonds. With it around her neck, she felt like Hawaiian royalty. Like Queen Liliuokalani.

"You are growing up full of aloha," Tutu Kane said. "And you are growing up so fast. Faster than David and Mary Lou, because of the war." Tutu Kane put his hands on Nanea's shoulders. "I gave them their leis when they each turned thirteen, not ten. But it is time for you to wear this." He hugged Nanea. "May it grant you a safe and peaceful journey through the rest of your life."

"Thank you," Nanea said. "Thank you everyone. For the gifts and for the birthday surprise."

David started strumming his ukulele, and Tutu Kane joined in. Everyone danced. Mary Lou and Dixie taught a new jitterbug step. Nanea giggled when Tutu tried it out.

"I think I should stick with hula," Tutu said, fanning her face.

"Hey!" Nanea exclaimed. "Everybody huddle up. I want to take a picture." Papa helped Nanea load the film into the camera as everyone gathered together.

Then she snapped a photo of the whole group. After that, Gene and Nanea switched places so that Nanea could be in a picture.

All too soon, the grown-ups began packing everything up to head home.

"What are you thinking?" David asked Nanea as he latched his instrument case.

Nanea put her new camera carefully back into the box. "I'm thinking that we are pretty lucky to be part of this 'ohana," Nanea answered.

David reached over and tugged a strand of Nanea's long dark hair. "Yes, we are. I never want to leave this place."

Nanea held those words in her heart. They were sweeter than her birthday cake. *David didn't want to leave! Never! So there, Uncle Sam!*

Nanea couldn't have asked for a better present.

BIG PROBLEMS

At the end of May, Nanea sat cross-legged on the living room floor with a sturdy canvas backpack in her lap. She was filling it with supplies. "I don't know why we need evacuation kits when everyone says the Japanese won't come back to attack us," she grumbled.

"The Army wants us all to have a bag packed," Mom said lightly. "In case of an emergency."

"But what kind of emergency?" Nanea asked.

"Oh, it's just part of being prepared." Mom motioned for Nanea to get back to work.

"Why doesn't Mary Lou have to make a kit?" Nanea asked.

"I already made mine," Mary Lou said, barely looking up from her knitting. "Four days' worth of supplies, as ordered."

Mom was working on her own kit.

"Where's David's?" Nanea asked. "And Papa's?"

"The Army only evacuates women and children," Mom said. "The men stay behind and help."

Nanea didn't like the sound of that. She thought of Donna's friends Emi and Susie going to the camps with their families. If Nanea had to leave her home for any reason, she wanted to go with everyone in her 'ohana.

"Let's not borrow trouble," Mom added. "We're doing this to be on the safe side. Nothing else is going to happen here."

"Don't you remember what Lieutenant Gregory told David?" Mary Lou interjected. "We're too far away for the Japanese to bother with anymore."

Nanea added some canned goods to her kit, which included a blanket, long pants and a sweater, a toothbrush and toothpaste, a hairbrush, soap, a towel, and a flashlight. She closed up the backpack and tried to strap it onto her back.

"Oof!" Nanea nearly tumbled backward. "How am I going to be able to carry all this *and* a gas mask?"

"And don't forget Mele's evacuation kit." Mary Lou pointed to the small bag Nanea had made for her dog.

"Do your best," Mom said. She rolled up some socks and slid them into her own evacuation kit.

Nanea reached into hers and pulled out two cans of peaches. She tried the backpack on again. "Much better," she said. She looked at the cans sadly. She really did love peaches.

There was a knock at the door. When Nanea opened it, Lily and Dixie were standing on the porch, and Lily was holding her bag of jacks.

"Want to play?" Lily asked.

Nanea was happy to leave thoughts of evacuation kits behind. Mom gave the girls some mountain apples. "Why don't you take them outside?" she suggested.

On the front porch, Mele wandered from girl to girl, hoping for a handout.

"I've never seen a dog eat apple before," Dixie said.

"Mele likes anything her people are eating," Nanea said. "Even green beans."

David's car rattled to a stop in front of the house. He waved to the girls as he hurried up the porch, an envelope in his hand. "Mail for you," he said to Nanea.

"A letter? From Donna?" she asked.

"You're fifty percent right," he said. "It's a letter, but

from Private First Class Ronald Paul." David made a
silly bow and then handed her the letter.

"Who?" Nanea turned the envelope over.

David winked. "Read it and see."

Nanea tore the letter open and read it aloud.

> *Dear Nanea,*
>
> *I hope you don't mind, but I asked your brother
> to deliver this to you. I'm healed up real well now,
> so Uncle Sam's putting me back to work. I ship out
> soon. But I couldn't leave without thanking you for
> letting me spend time with Mele. She was better than
> any medicine they gave me in the hospital, I can tell
> you that for sure.*
>
> *Well, as you say in Hawaii, aloha.*
> *PFC Ronald Paul*

Below that, he'd signed, *"Tennessee."*

"Neat," Lily said.

"Good job, Monkey." David ruffled Nanea's hair.
"And you too, pup," he called to Mele as he headed into
the house.

Nanea sat down on the front step and read the letter

again. "This gives me an idea," she said to Lily and Dixie. "Something different for the Hula Dog act."

"It's pretty popular," Lily said, sitting down on one side of Nanea.

"Mele really cheers people up," Dixie said, sitting down on the other side of Nanea.

"Well, what if I took Mele to visit sick and injured servicemen?" Nanea asked. "We could dance, sure, but they could also pet her and stuff like that." Nanea tapped the letter against her leg. "Tennessee said spending time with Mele was better than any medicine the hospital gave him. This could be Operation Mele Medicine!"

Dixie tugged on her ear. "That sounds good for the soldiers," she began cautiously. "But I remember when I got my tonsils out. My friends couldn't come in because they weren't fourteen yet. Hospitals are very strict about who can visit."

"We're not fourteen," Lily said.

"And she's a dog," Dixie said, pointing at Mele.

Nanea rested her chin in her hands. "Those are two big problems," she agreed. "There has to be some way to solve them. I wonder—"

But Nanea stopped talking. She heard David and Papa in the living room, and there was an urgency to David's voice that made her listen.

"Something is up," David was saying. "I've never seen so many troops walking around downtown. There are ships as far as the eye can see off Waikiki. And I heard there's lots of activity at Hickam Field, too."

Nanea hugged her knees close. Little prickles of worry raced up and down her body.

"The scuttlebutt I hear is that it's for something in the Pacific," Papa said. "Not here. Maybe Midway."

"Daddy and Gene were talking about Midway last night," Lily whispered. "The United States has a base there, but the Japanese want to control it, they said."

"I wish I was out there," David said. "I feel so useless delivering messages."

"Delivering messages is important work," Papa assured him.

"When I join up, I'll be able to do something that matters," David replied.

"What you're doing right now matters," Papa insisted. "We don't know what's happening in Midway yet." Papa's voice faded as he and David left the room.

Nanea couldn't breathe. It had been a long time since David mentioned joining the Army. Nanea had hoped he'd forgotten about it. Now she knew there was no chance he would forget. This was an even bigger big problem.

There was an assembly at school the next day. In the auditorium, a row of chairs marched across each side of the stage, with a tall wooden podium in the middle. The student War Stamps monitors from each class sat on one side. Nanea and Lily waved to Dixie. She gave a tiny wave back. Principal Baxter and several special guests, including Lieutenant Gregory, sat on the other side of the podium.

"This is boring." Billy Cruz wiggled around in the seat next to Nanea. "With a capital B."

"Remember your manners, please, Billy," Miss Smith said.

Billy let out a big sigh when another adult got up to speak. Miss Smith gave him a stern look.

Nanea had to admit, there was a lot of talking.

Finally, Mrs. Baxter returned to the podium.

"Thank you so much for those words, Mr. Ross," the principal said. "And now, for our final speaker of the assembly—"

Nanea's class applauded loudly as Lieutenant Gregory walked to the podium. He thanked Mrs. Baxter. "I am honored to be here today and proud of your patriotic support of your country. You have truly shown the aloha spirit through your participation in the War Stamps drive. This school alone has collected enough money to buy one tank! Think of that." Lieutenant Gregory looked out over the auditorium, smiling.

"From this young first-grader here in the front row," he pointed at a girl wearing a big red bow in her hair, "to the President of the United States, every person's contribution matters. Whether you buy a stamp, invite a soldier to dinner, or loan your dog to good old Uncle Sam . . ." With those words, Lieutenant Gregory seemed to look right at Nanea.

Nanea slunk down in her seat. Why did he have to bring up the part about dogs?

". . . what you do counts, so keep it up!" Lieutenant Gregory finished. He snapped off a salute to the students. "Now, one class has earned a Minuteman flag with their dedicated support of the War Stamps drive." He stepped away from the podium, picked up a folded flag, and paused, scanning the chairs where the War Stamps monitors were sitting. "Miss Dixie Moreno, please come forward and accept this for Miss Smith's third-grade class!"

Dixie squealed and jumped up, stumbling in her excitement to cross the stage. Nanea looked over at Miss Smith and saw tears glistening in her eyes. Nanea's classmates whistled and cheered, and the principal didn't even shush them.

Nanea cheered, too, because she was so happy for Dixie and Miss Smith and their class. But inside, she was unhappy for herself. Lieutenant Gregory's words reminded her that she stood a good chance of losing both her brother and her dog to the war.

David's Birthday

CHAPTER 17

How does this look?" Dixie held out a flower arrangement she'd made.

"Beautiful," Nanea said without looking.

Dixie's smile faded. "You don't like it," she muttered.

"Yes, I *do* like it," Nanea insisted. "I'm sorry, Dixie. I'm just distracted."

That morning, Nanea had overheard her parents talking. Mom had sounded so upset. "I'm worried that he'll go right out and enlist," Mom had said. "He's eighteen today. We can't stop him." Then Mom had started to cry.

Papa's calm voice had answered, "Let's not borrow trouble, May. Besides, today is for celebrating David." Then their voices had dropped off, and Nanea couldn't hear anything more.

Nanea told her friends what her parents had said.

Lily sighed. "The war sure has put a dark cloud over a lot of birthday luaus."

"Remember what your dad said," Dixie encouraged. "Today is a day to celebrate David."

"I'll try." Nanea looked around the lanai and the backyard. "There's still a lot to do to get ready. Let's hang the streamers."

Dixie yawned. "I'll help," she said.

"Did your cousin wet the bed again last night?" Lily asked.

Dixie nodded as she sniffed the air. "But that *kalua* pig smells so good that I can forget all about being tired." She rubbed her stomach. "I've hardly eaten any-thing all day, just waiting for this!"

Food was an important part of any luau. Nanea loved the festive dishes, especially Tutu's poi. There would be *lomi* salmon with tomatoes and onions, *laulau*—pork and butterfish wrapped in ti leaves—and of course the special recipe that the luau was named after: chicken and taro leaves baked with coconut milk. But more than the food, Nanea especially loved know-ing that people in her 'ohana had been celebrating like this since she didn't even know how long. In ancient times, men and women couldn't eat together. She was glad that had changed. Otherwise, she wouldn't be able to attend her own big brother's birthday party!

"My mom's bringing three coconut cream pies." Lily stretched to hang one end of a pair of streamers in the mango tree. "Here, grab that end," she said to Dixie.

"So 'ono!" Dixie sighed, grabbing the streamers. "Okay, where does this go?" she asked.

"Over there." Lily pointed to the banana tree on the other side of the yard. "It's going to be a great party."

After Nanea carried the step stool to Dixie, she sat down in the grass next to Mele. "What are we going to do about Operation Mele Medicine?" she asked, stroking her dog's ear. "How can we get you into the hospitals to cheer up wounded soldiers?"

Mele only thumped her tail.

Dixie secured the streamers and climbed off the stool. "Maybe you need a new approach," she suggested. "Don't you remember Lieutenant Gregory saying there are lots of ways to help Uncle Sam?"

"Wait a minute," Lily said. "Nanea, why don't you tell *Lieutenant Gregory* about your idea for Operation Mele Medicine? Maybe he could help."

Nanea felt a twist in her stomach. "I can't," she said. "Lieutenant Gregory wants me to give Mele up for Dogs for Defense," she blurted out.

Lily and Dixie were shocked. They hurried over to Nanea and sat down, too.

"When did he say that?" Lily asked.

"He's *always* asking about Mele and telling me what a smart dog she is. Remember that night at dinner?" Nanea asked. She listed all the other times Lieutenant Gregory had told her the Army needed smart dogs. "And last week at the assembly, when he brought up Dogs for Defense, he looked right at me." Nanea bit her lip to keep from crying. "I am not going to give up David *and* Mele."

Nanea's friends were quiet. Then Dixie sat up straight. "Maybe if you tell Lieutenant Gregory about Operation Mele Medicine, he would see that's a better way for Mele to help the war effort. Maybe he would even talk to someone at the hospitals and convince them to let Mele in."

"He is good at convincing people to do things," Lily agreed. "Remember the War Stamps talk?"

Nanea nodded. But she just didn't know if she could

trust Lieutenant Gregory to help her. "I have to think about it," she said.

"Sit down, please, everyone," Tutu called out later that afternoon. "We'll have some hula in honor of David's special day."

Tutu Kane played his ukulele while Nanea and Mary Lou danced the hula they'd created to celebrate David. Nanea felt proud of the way it turned out. The dance told the story of her wonderful big brother. Nanea's hands and feet talked about all David had done and all he would do. She and Mary Lou chose movements to compare him to the tallest of palm trees: so strong, but able to bend in a hard wind. Each step put more distance between Nanea and her worries. After they finished, Tutu and Mom danced, too. Nanea hoped someday she would be as graceful as her mother and grandmother.

"Wonderful!" Lieutenant Gregory exclaimed when they finished. He turned to Papa. "It's an honor to be part of this special day." As Mom joined their conversation, Lieutenant Gregory said, "Everything was delicious, Mrs. Mitchell."

Mom smiled. "Can I get you another slice of pie?"

Lieutenant Gregory groaned. "Maybe just a sliver."

Dixie ran over to Nanea and Lily. "You'll never guess!" She jumped up and down. "My dad was just talking to Donna's dad. Mr. Hill has invited us to live at his house until Donna and Mrs. Hill come home. I'll have my own room!" She clasped her hands together. "I can sleep again!"

"That's great news," Lily said.

"I'm so happy for you," added Nanea.

Mom handed a plate to Nanea. "Could you please take this to Lieutenant Gregory?" she asked.

"Now's the time to talk to him," Lily urged.

"You can do it," Dixie added.

Nanea stood tall as she and Lily and Dixie approached the lieutenant.

He took the plate. "You three look so serious. What's up?"

Nanea grabbed hands with Lily and Dixie and took a deep breath. "I want Mele to help Uncle Sam."

"Dogs for Defense?" Lieutenant Gregory paused with a bite of pie halfway to his mouth. He sounded surprised. "I know how much Mele means to you—and how you've already lost her once."

Nanea was surprised. "You do?"

Lieutenant Gregory put his fork down. "The first thing David told me about his baby sister was how determined she was to find her dog." He smiled warmly at Nanea. "You didn't give up on Mele. We both admire you for that."

"But we thought you wanted Mele for Dogs for Defense!" Lily said.

"What gave you that idea?" Lieutenant Gregory asked.

"You were so interested in her that night at dinner," Dixie explained.

Lieutenant Gregory laughed. "Who wouldn't be interested in a hula-dancing dog?"

"So you don't want Mele to join the Army?" Nanea asked, squeezing her friends' hands.

"Not if you don't want her to. Dogs for Defense is an important program, but it's your decision to make. Not mine." He smiled again. "Besides, it seems she already has a big job. I hear that the soldiers love Hula Dog."

Relief washed over Nanea like a wave. "I have an idea about that," she said. "It's called Operation Mele Medicine." She told him about the letter from Tennessee. "I could take Mele to the hospitals once a week so the men could pet her and play with her."

Lieutenant Gregory frowned. "Dogs and hospitals don't exactly mix."

"Well, she doesn't have to be *in* the hospital," Nanea said. "She could be on the lawn, and the men could go to her."

Lieutenant Gregory's mouth opened, then closed. He lifted up a finger, and then put it down. He shook his head. "You've got this all worked out, haven't you?"

"Almost." Nanea paused. "Would you talk to the hospitals? They won't listen to a kid like me."

Lieutenant Gregory raised one eyebrow, and then he burst out laughing. "I'm sure glad you're on our side," he said. "Otherwise, we wouldn't have a chance in the world of winning this war." He stuck his hand out to shake Nanea's. "You've got a deal, Miss Mitchell."

VICTORY!

CHAPTER 18

Nanea!" Mary Lou shook her. "Wake up!"

Nanea bolted out of bed. She grabbed her evacuation kit, Mele's evacuation kit, and Mele. "Do we have to leave?" she asked, her heart racing. "Did the attack come?"

"Come on!" Mary Lou called as she hurried out of the room.

With Mele and the evacuation kits still in her arms, Nanea followed her sister to the living room. Their parents were gathered around the Philco radio. Nanea dropped the kits and sat on the floor next to Mom, Mele on her lap.

"Aloha, fellow Americans on this fine day, June sixth, 1942. This is Owen Cunningham with Captain Buckner, an eyewitness to the battle. Captain Buckner, will you set the stage for us?

Yes. As the enemy approached, we saw our fighters begin to engage them. Several went down in flames. Our heavy ground fire was too hot for them. All in all, the attack lasted about one half hour."

"Finally, some good news!" Mom patted her chest, exhaling loudly.

"We can all take a deep breath," Papa said. "Hawaii doesn't have to worry about more attacks."

Nanea was confused. "What does this mean?"

"We won!" Mary Lou got up and jitterbugged around the room. "We won the Battle of Midway!"

"This calls for pancakes!" Mom said.

Mary Lou went to help her.

Nanea kept her arms around Mele. A million questions bounced around her brain. *Did this mean the end of blackouts? Of curfews? Would things finally go back to normal?* But then she realized something wonderful: *If the battle was over, David wouldn't need to join the Army! Everything was going to be all right!*

At breakfast, Nanea poured syrup over a second stack of pancakes.

Mom laughed. "You have a good appetite today!"

"The war is over!" Nanea cried, picking up her fork.

Papa set down his coffee cup. "Well, Sunshine, this is good news, that's for sure. But the war isn't over."

"But Mary Lou said we won." Nanea felt like she'd been splashed in the face with icy water.

Papa nodded. "Yes. We won a very important battle. It's the first time the Japanese Navy has been stopped in the Pacific. Now our Navy has the advantage instead of theirs."

"I don't understand," Nanea said, putting her fork down. Before she could ask any more questions, David came in the back door. Everyone turned to look at him.

"Have you heard?" Nanea asked.

David nodded. "Victory at Midway! It's great news."

"I'm happy for Uncle Sam, but I'm mostly happy for us," Nanea said.

"Why is that?" David asked.

"Because now you won't have to go in the Army! Our lauhala family, remember?"

David cleared his throat. "You know nothing can break the ties of this 'ohana, right? Nothing. Not even if one of us goes far away."

A cold feeling crept over Nanea.

"Mom, Pop." David stood tall. "You're looking at the

newest member of the United States Army."

"No!" Nanea screamed.

Mary Lou hugged her. "Shh. Shh."

"So you've enlisted," Papa said.

"Pop, I've known all along I would enlist. This business in Midway just sealed the deal." David pulled a chair up to the table. "We need fresh recruits if we're going to win the war. I can't stand by, watching from the sidelines anymore."

Mom wrung her apron hem. "Did Lieutenant Gregory talk you into this?"

"No," David answered. "It's my decision. All the way." He rested his arm on Mom's shoulder. "I waited until after my birthday because you all were working so hard to make it special. But this is something I needed to do."

The room was so quiet that Nanea could hear the second hand moving on the kitchen clock.

"Well, then." Papa stood. He clapped David on the shoulder. "We're proud of you, son."

Mom wiped her eyes. "When do you leave?" she asked.

"I ship out in three weeks," David answered.

Nanea pushed her plate away. "I hate the Army," she said under her breath. Then she started to cry.

"Nanea!" Mom scolded. "We don't say hate."

It was hard to give a stink eye through tears, but Nanea tried. She glowered at David.

"Hey, look at it this way." David grinned. "You and Mary Lou won't have to share a bedroom anymore. You can each have your own."

"I like sharing a bedroom." Nanea wiped her damp cheeks. She knew David was trying to make her feel better. But she was so sad. And mad. Mad enough that she didn't even want to talk to David. Maybe not ever again.

"It'll be okay," David said. "I'll be okay." He knocked on his head. "Hard as a coconut shell." He flexed his biceps. "And strong as a shark."

Nanea stood up. "I'm going for a walk," she announced.

Both her bad mood and Mele followed her out the door and down the street. She didn't realize where she was going until she found herself at her grandparents'. Instead of going inside, she marched around the house to the back garden where Tutu grew flowers for her dancers' leis. Nanea began to jerk weeds out of the ground, one after another, growing angrier by the minute. She threw the weeds this way and that. Finally, all the mad inside bubbled over and spilled out of her.

"I hate him!" she yelled, tears rolling down her cheeks. She didn't care what Mom said. She had never been so mad at her brother in her whole life. It just wasn't fair. Their family was doing so much for the war effort. Papa worked extra shifts. Mom taught first aid. Mary Lou cooked and served meals. Nanea thought about how she'd performed at USO shows and worked hard to win a Minuteman flag. Then there were all the things the Honolulu Helpers had done for Uncle Sam— not to mention Operation Mele Medicine. Why wasn't that enough?

"Nanea?" Tutu stood there, looking concerned.

Nanea ducked her head so Tutu wouldn't see that she was crying. "I thought I could do some weeding for you," she said.

"Oh?" Tutu took in the weeds all over the yard. "I see. How about if we get a bucket and pick those up?"

As they worked in silence, the rhythm of tossing the weeds in the bucket calmed Nanea down a bit.

"Much better," Tutu said when they had finished. "Come sit." She motioned Nanea to follow her to the lanai.

Nanea told Tutu the news.

"Oh, keiki." Tutu patted her ample lap, and Nanea crawled into it. "I didn't know." She held Nanea close. "Our hearts can cry together."

They sat for some time, Nanea breathing in Tutu's familiar smells of coconut and coffee. After a while, Tutu Kane joined them, and Tutu quietly told him about David.

"The war has brought many changes, but this is the biggest change of all," Tutu Kane said with a sigh. He looked at Nanea. "You know I gave your brother his Hawaiian name, right?"

Nanea nodded.

"It is a big responsibility, bestowing a name. But the minute I saw David, I was reminded of my own grandfather. David had his eyes, his nose, his determined mouth. And there wasn't a braver man than Kekoa Pono." Tutu Kane shook his head.

"David is brave," Nanea said. "He tackles waves that make other surfers stay on the beach."

"And you know the most important part of bravery?" Tutu asked.

"Strong muscles?" Nanea asked.

Tutu smiled. "Well, one strong muscle." She patted her chest. "David has a brave heart. Like you, I wish he could have made another decision. But I know he is doing what he thinks is right for his 'ohana and his country. That is true courage."

Nanea wiped at her wet face again. "I don't want David to get hurt," she whispered. It scared her to say those words.

Tutu Kane shook his head. "You have had to grow up too fast because of this war."

Nanea touched her shell necklace. That was what Tutu Kane had said when he'd given it to her.

"Aloha," Tutu said. "Love is what carries us through times like these."

The three of them sat together in the warm sun, listening to a pair of zebra doves making their rapid-fire calls from the mango tree. Nanea took a shaky breath, filling her lungs with the sweet scents of the ginger and the tuberoses and the carnations.

"Tutu? May I ask a favor?"

"Anything," Tutu answered.

Nanea pointed to the flower garden. "May I cut some of those when David leaves? I want to make him a lei."

GOOD-BYES AND GOOD DEEDS

hree weeks passed quickly, and then it was time for David to leave for boot camp in Mississippi. Nanea wasn't able to keep back the tears when she presented David with the lei she'd made. "Promise to throw it overboard," she demanded.

"I will, Monkey." He ruffled her hair. "But I don't need to. You can bet your bottom dollar that I'll be coming back."

Nanea's weren't the only tears as the 'ohana said their good-byes. Even Papa's eyes glistened as they waited at the fence by the dock while David marched up the steps to the pier with the other recruits.

Nanea waved to David until he was smaller than one of the shells on her necklace. And she kept waving as the boat steamed out of sight.

"We'd better get going," Papa said. "You have an important job."

"Are you sure you're up for this today?" Mom asked.

Nanea nodded. "It'll be good to have something to take my mind off David's leaving."

Shortly after they got back home, Dixie and Lily arrived. "We're here to help," Dixie said.

"I'll fill the washtub," offered Lily.

"I'll get Mele," said Nanea.

"What shall I do?" asked Dixie.

"Be ready with the hose!" Nanea called.

Together, the three girls scrubbed Mele from nose to tail. They rubbed her dry with towels, fluffing up her fur.

"She looks better than Lassie," Dixie said.

"But we look like drowned rats!" Lily tugged at her soaking-wet blouse. "I'm running home to change."

"Me, too! Back in a jiff." Dixie ran off to her new home at the Hills' house.

Soon they were back, and all three girls were dry and spiffed up. Nanea held tight to her 'eke hula.

"Are you ready?" Papa asked.

"Yes," Nanea nodded.

"Me, too," Dixie said, holding Mary Lou's record player in her arms.

"Not quite." Lily set down the records she was holding and pulled a hair ribbon from her pocket. She tied it around Mele's neck. "Now we're ready."

Lieutenant Gregory greeted them at the hospital. "The men are waiting for you in the day room," he said.

A few moments later, a no-nonsense nurse stopped them in the hall. "Where are you going?" she asked in a voice as starched as her white hat.

"Um," Nanea hesitated.

"Is there a problem, nurse?" Lieutenant Gregory asked.

"No dogs allowed." She sniffed as if Mele had rolled in dead fish. "And no children, either," she said.

Lieutenant Gregory looked left. He looked right. "Dog?" He scratched his head. "All I see is a four-legged hula dancer," he said.

The nurse frowned. Then she shook her head. "Hula dancer, indeed. I hope you have permission." She put her hands on her hips.

Lieutenant Gregory brought out a piece of paper. "We do."

The nurse scanned it. "What is this world coming to?" she grumbled. But she waved them on.

"Mahalo," Nanea said. She wasn't sure the nurse heard her.

"There it is." Lieutenant Gregory nodded at a door at the far end of the hall.

Nanea paused. She thought about how she hadn't liked Lieutenant Gregory at first. Who would have thought he would have worked so hard to help put Operation Mele Medicine into place? He had pulled a lot of strings and gotten them into a room inside the hospital.

Mele tugged at her leash, looking at Nanea as if she was saying, *Well, what are we waiting for?*

"There's a room over there where you can change," Lieutenant Gregory said.

Nanea quickly put on her dance costume and then she tied Mele's on, too. Lily adjusted Nanea's *lei'opo.* Dixie fluffed her skirt.

"Ready?" Lily asked.

Nanea took a deep breath. She thought of David,

her brave brother. With another deep breath, she straightened her shoulders and stepped into the day room. It was full of wounded men who needed some Mele medicine.

When Dixie put on the first record, Mele wagged her tail. Nanea knew the two of them had an important story to tell. A story of aloha. A story of healing.

She lifted her hands to her heart. "Let's dance, Hula Dog!"

And they did.

INSIDE Nanea's World

The Battle of Midway was not the end of World War Two, but it was an important turning point—especially for the people of Hawaii. American forces defeated the Japanese Navy at Midway Island. Much of the tension and fear that Nanea and her neighbors had been feeling was lifted, because Hawaii was no longer on constant alert for enemy attacks.

Life, however, was not back to normal. The rules of martial law, such as curfews and blackouts, still applied. The worries of war still hung over the island. People did all they could to help, but many were frustrated that they couldn't do more. This was especially true for Americans of Japanese ancestry. Many of them were eager to defend their country and tried enlisting in the military. Young men like Gene were told they could not serve. They were considered "enemy aliens."

Although Nanea's story is fictional, the group that Gene organizes—the Varsity Victory Volunteers—was a real group formed by college students. They built roads, dug ammunition pits, and hauled stones. Their tireless work was testament to their loyalty to America. In 1943, the military allowed Japanese Americans to enlist. President Roosevelt fully supported the change, writing, "Americanism is a matter of the mind and heart; Americanism is not, and never was, a matter of race or ancestry." The Army hoped for 1,500 volunteers from Hawaii. They were stunned when nearly 10,000

Americans of Japanese ancestry signed up.

Younger students were also committed to helping. Many joined church groups or clubs, like the Junior Red Cross, to roll bandages, make food packages, or knit sweaters and socks for soldiers. Girls like Nanea started their own clubs. All across the country, kids did their part to help America win the war.

The people of Hawaii did more than their part when it came to buying War Stamps. These stamps weren't used for mailing letters. They were a way to lend money to the government, which used the funds to buy war equipment. Kids bought ten-cent stamps at school. Each stamp was placed in a special booklet that the whole class shared. When the booklet was full, the class bought a War Bond for $18.75. Kids used their allowances or the money they earned from weekend jobs to buy War Stamps. Some even went without milk at lunch, using that money to "Back the Attack."

Hawaii's patriotism set records. There were more War Bonds purchased in Hawaii than anywhere else in the country. The government set sales goals, and island-ers went above and beyond those goals all four years of the war. The fact that the people of Hawaii had wit-nessed the war firsthand contributed to their dedicated support of America's troops. But the spirit of aloha and the deeply held belief in kokua had much to do with their generosity.

GLOSSARY of Hawaiian Words

ae *(AYE)*—yes, agreement

aloha *(ah-LO-hah)*—hello, good-bye, love, compassion

'ami *(AH-mee)*—a movement in hula in which the hips rotate in a circular motion

'eke hula *(EH-kay HOO-la)*—a bag or basket used to carry hula implements and costumes

hala *(HAH-lah)*—a large tree with pineapple-shaped fruit or fragrant flowers

holoku *(ho-loh-KOO)*—a floor-length formal gown with a train

kaholo *(ka-HO-loh)*—a side-to-side movement in hula

kalua *(kah-LOO-ah)*—to bake in an underground oven

keiki *(KAY-kee)*—child

kokua *(KOH-KOO-ah)*—assistance, a good deed, to help

kumu hula *(KOO-moo HOO-lah)*—hula teacher

kupe'e *(KOO-peh-eh)*—an ankle decoration

lanai *(LAH-nye)*—covered porch

lauhala *(LAH-ooh-HAH-lah)*—the leaf of the hala tree; used to make baskets and other woven items

laulau *(LAH-ooh-LAH-ooh)*—a dish of fish with chicken, pork, or beef wrapped in ti or taro leaves

lei *(LAY)*—a wreath of flowers, feathers, or shells worn around the neck or head

lei po'o *(LAY POH-oh)*—a wreath of flowers, feathers, or shells worn on the head

lele *(LEH-leh)*—a forward-and-back movement in hula

lomi *(LOH-mee)*—a dish of salmon, tomatoes, and onions that is served cold

luau *(LOO-ow)*—a party or feast that includes entertainment—often traditional Hawaiian music and hula

mahalo *(mah-HAH-loh)*—thank you

mahalo ia 'oe *(mah-HAH-loh yah OYE)*—another form of thank you

makaukau *(MAH-kow-KOW)*—ready, prepared

mauka *(MAH-OOH-kah)*—the side facing the mountain

mele *(MEH-leh)*—song

Ni'ihau *(NEE-ee-HAH-ooh)*—one of the eight main islands of Hawaii

'ohana *(oh-HAH-nah)*—family

'ono *(OH-no)*—tasty, delicious

pikake *(PEE-KAH-keh)*—jasmine flower

poi *(POY)*—a starchy pudding made from pounded taro root. A *poi dog* is a mixed-breed dog, named for a now-extinct breed that was fed poi.

pu'ili *(pooh-EE-lee)*—bamboo sticks used as hula instruments

taro *(TAIR-oh)*—a tropical plant with a starchy, edible root

tutu *(TOO-too)*—grandparent, usually grandmother

tutu kane *(TOO-too KAH-nay)*—grandfather

Read more of NANEA'S stories,

available from booksellers and at *americangirl.com*

❀ *Classics* ❀

Nanea's classic series in two volumes:

Volume 1:
Growing Up with Aloha

Nanea may be the youngest in
her family, but she *knows* she's
ready for more responsibility.
When Japan attacks Pearl
Harbor and America goes to
war, Nanea is faced with
grown-up chores and choices.

Volume 2:
Hula for the Home Front

The war has changed everything in Nanea's world. She's
trying to do her part, but it's
not easy to make sacrifices.
Hula, and a surprising dance
partner, help Nanea hold on to
her aloha spirit.

❀ *Journey in Time* ❀

Travel back in time—and spend a few days with Nanea!

Prints in the Sand

Step into Nanea's world of Hawaii during World War Two.
Learn how to dance a hula. Help a lost dog. Work in a
Victory Garden, or send secret messages for the war effort.
Choose your own path through this multiple-ending story.

❀ A Sneak Peek at ❀

Prints in the Sand

My Journey with Nanea

Meet Nanea and take a journey back in time in a
book that lets *you* decide what happens.

Overseas. That's where Dad is. So if I look far enough out to sea, will I find him there?

I shade my eyes and gaze past the beach where my little brothers build their sand castle, out to the blurred line of the horizon. There, I see a glimmer of light. I imagine it's Dad's plane coming home, dipping its wing to say *aloha* to me.

Being away from Dad is so hard! My dad is in the army, but we've *always* moved with him from base to base. That's how we came to Oahu six months ago.

Then, at the start of summer, Dad was sent to Iraq, and Mom said it was too dangerous for us to go along. *If it's so dangerous,* I wanted to ask, *why is Dad going?*

But I didn't ask. And we never talk about Iraq. We just say that Dad is "overseas," like he's on vacation somewhere. And I pretend that my mom, brothers, and I are, too. Because Hawaii just doesn't feel like home— not without Dad.

A squeal cuts through the air. It's my brother Alex. His twin, Aidan, is chasing him with a cup of water. I'm about to tell the boys to settle down when someone else steps in—Auntie Ona, our new babysitter.

At least someone's having fun here, I think as I

straighten out my towel. My twin brothers usually do have fun, maybe because they always have each other. *But who do I have now that Dad's gone?*

I had my friend Kayla in California. Mom wants me to make new friends, but what good is making friends if I just have to leave them behind the *next* time we move?

At least I have Nancy Drew, I remind myself, blowing the sand off the cover of my new mystery. I crack open the book and try to read, but some delicious smell drifts out of Auntie Ona's basket. I'm pretty sure it's her amazing guava bread, which she baked for our picnic dinner. Yum!

It's sure hard to concentrate with that bread so close. Plus, the sounds of the beach are distracting. Birds chirp, waves splash onto shore, kids squeal and bark. *Wait, what?*

I roll onto my hip to look for the dog. I love Nancy Drew, but I love dogs even more! I've begged Mom to get one, but she says there are enough bodies in the house to take care of without adding one more.

Just beyond a few bright beach umbrellas, I see a salt-and-pepper tail bobbing back and forth. I can't see the dog's head, but a spray of sand tells me that it's digging for something.

I hop up to get a closer look.

As I walk past the rainbow of umbrellas, I can see the dog better. It has scruffy fur and floppy ears. The dog wears a pretty green collar with little flowers on it. It must be a she—and she belongs to someone. Her head disappears into the hole, and when it pops back out, something dangles from her mouth.

"What did you find there, girl?" As I take a step toward her, she sticks her rump in the air. She races in a little circle. Then she stops, her body tense, waiting for me to make my move.

"Oh, so you want to play?" I call to her, laughing.

She drops whatever she's holding and barks. Then she takes off running toward the pink hotel next door. It's *really* pink, like the strawberry shave ice I get from the stand on the beach. I'm blinded for a second by all that pink, and when I look for the dog again, she's gone. But what did she leave behind for me? I stoop to pick it up. It looks like a pile of shells, but when I lift one, they all come with it. It's a necklace!

"That looks like an old *puka* shell necklace," says a woman sitting under a candy-apple red umbrella. Her little girl is asleep in the shade.

"Really?" I say, examining the necklace.

"That's very special," the woman explains. "Puka necklaces were given to people setting off on long journeys—to assure a safe and peaceful voyage. Are you taking a trip soon?"

Not until Dad comes home, I think.

Another shrill bark catches my ear. This one comes from the patio of the pink hotel. A black nose pokes out from beneath the ruffle of a tablecloth. The dog barks again. Is she talking to me? I have to follow her!

I glance back at my brothers, who are stacking cups of sand on top of one another to form a wobbly tower. Auntie Ona helps balance it as Alex adds a sixth cup. They'll be fine without me. I check my watch, which reads 3:22. There's plenty of time before dinner. Plenty of time to follow that dog. So with a tingle of excitement, I hurry toward the patio. The puka shells jingle in my hand. I don't want to lose them, so I slide the necklace carefully over my head. But as I pull my hair out from under the string of shells, the ground drops from beneath my feet. I feel the whoosh of an ocean breeze. And then a pink mist covers my eyes . . .

I'm still standing—on wobbly legs. And that pink mist is the hotel in front of me. But now there's some-thing else: a barbed-wire fence. It stretches along the beach as far as my eyes can see. That wasn't here before!

Running along the fence are paw prints—*dog* prints. They lead me a few feet to the right, and then they disappear. Did the dog go under the barbed wire? When I kneel beside the fence, I spot a hole. It's big enough for a girl to fit through.

Without even thinking, I duck through the hole and follow the paw prints around to the front of the hotel. But a buzz of low voices near the entrance surprises me. Glancing up, I see a crowd of soldiers and sailors. Why are they all at the beach—dressed in uniform?

Ooga! A shiny, navy blue car inches slowly through the crowd. It looks like the old-time cars I've seen in parades sometimes. When the door opens, I'm surprised to see a nurse pop out. She wears a stiff white cap, and as she straightens up, I see the red cross sewn to her starched white dress.

As she hurries into the hotel and that old car rumbles away, anxiety rumbles through my stomach, too. Something's not quite right here. *Soldiers? Nurses? Old-time cars? Why are they all here at the beach?*

Then I see a girl step out of the crowd—someone my own age, finally! She wears a bright red flower in her dark, wavy hair. She raises her hand to her mouth and calls, "*Mele!*"

Then a furry bundle of energy pops out of a patch of flowers. It's my dog! *Her dog,* I correct myself. *And her name must be Mele!*

The girl scoops up the pup and disappears back into the hotel, so I follow her. I'm three steps into the lobby before I realize, with embarrassment, that I'm still wearing my swimsuit. Do I have time to run back to the beach and grab my cover-up?

I hurry back outside, dodge a few soldiers, and race through the sand toward the beach. But suddenly, I'm not sure which way to go.

Find the red umbrella, I tell myself. It was the

brightest thing on the beach. There it is!

I dart toward it, but as I round the umbrella, I know right away that this isn't the same one. Instead of a woman smiling up at me, a sailor sits cross-legged on a towel. He tips his white hat at me and grins.

I run past him, toward the water. My brothers should be easy enough to find—or hear. But one look at the shoreline tells me that *they're* gone, too!

There are two women on the beach, but they're wearing old-fashioned suits with skirts attached. One has a funny rubber cap on her head. *I don't know anyone here,* I realize. *I don't even know where "here" is—or when. It's like I've traveled back in time!* A shiver of excitement runs down my spine.

I take a deep breath and try to retrace my steps. I remember spotting the dog and getting up from my towel. I found the puka shell necklace and put it on, and . . . then what? It all seems like a hazy dream.

As I reach up to touch the necklace, the puka shells feel smooth and mysterious. I slide the necklace off to take a closer look. That's when the ground beneath me rolls again, like a surfboard on a rising wave . . .

About the Author

KIRBY LARSON is the author of several
novels, including the Newbery Honor
book *Hattie Big Sky*, and *Dash*, winner of the
Scott O'Dell Award for Historical Fiction.
With her friend Mary Nethery, she has
written two award-winning picture books.
She lives in Kenmore, Washington, with
her husband and Winston the wonder dog.
In her free time, she hunts for beach glass
and tidbits from history that she can turn
into stories for young readers. Visit Kirby at
www.kirbylarson.com.